FOXBROOKE EXTRAS

EVIE ALEXANDER

EMLIN
PRESS

First Published in Great Britain 2024 by Emlin Press

ISBN (eBook) 978-1-914473-57-9

ISBN (Print) 978-1-914473-58-6

A CIP catalogue record for this book is available from the British Library.

www.emlinpress.com

For you, my fabulous reader. Thank you for being here!

ALSO BY EVIE ALEXANDER

THE KINLOCH SERIES

Highland Games

Hollywood Games

Kissing Games

Musical Games

Wedding Games

Christmas Games

THE FOXBROOKE SERIES

One Night in Foxbrooke

Love ad Lib

An Unholy Affair

The Upper Crush

The Love Position

Christmas off Script

One Night Only

Righting Mr Wrong

Under the Influencer

Foxbrooke Extras

ABOUT FOXBROOKE EXTRAS

Dear gorgeous reader,

Welcome to Foxbrooke Extras! This is the place you'll find the prequel novella, One Night in Foxbrooke, as well as the extended epilogues for Love ad Lib, An Unholy Affair, The Upper Crush, The Love Position, and Christmas off Script.

These are already available free for newsletter subscribers, but this is the first time they've been collated into one place in eBook and print!

Enjoy, and huge love and hugs,

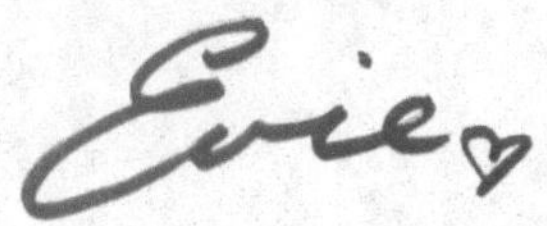

I

ONE NIGHT IN FOXBROOKE

'Thank god you're here.'

Leia's mother, Jan, the cook at Foxbrooke Manor, held her tightly in a fierce hug.

Leia smelled garlic, tomato, basil and the slight hint of desperation on her mother's apron. She disengaged before emotion got the better of her.

'Well, it's not like I've got anything else in the calendar today,' she replied, pasting on a smile.

Jan's face fell. 'I'm so sorry, love.'

The two women stared at each other as invisible words, thoughts and feelings ricocheted between them.

Leia shrugged.

'Love—'

'Words won't change anything, Mum,' she interrupted, unbuttoning her coat. 'Let's focus on the task in hand. How bad is it?'

Jan blew out her cheeks and glanced up at the grand facade of the manor. 'Pardon my French, but it's a shitshow.'

'Isn't that what passes as a normal day around here?'

Her mother rolled her eyes as she pushed the door open.

Leia followed her down the corridor towards the manor's kitchens, the slap of their footsteps on the stone floor accompanying her mother's rapid-fire speech.

'It's always a bit crazy working here, but this bloody bug that's going around has screwed everything up.' Her mother shook her head. 'Most of the staff here are off sick, all the temp staff from the agency I had lined up are down with it and Luke and your dad can't help as they're just as short-staffed at the factory.' She shot Leia a look, her brow furrowed. 'We've got a dinner of a hundred to cater and half the ingredients are missing because the bloody delivery company doesn't have enough drivers.'

Leia swallowed. The Duke of Somerset was a true foodie. This wasn't good.

'It's okay, Mum. We can improvise.'

Her mother nodded, her breath almost matching the speed of her pace. Leia couldn't remember ever seeing her this stressed before.

'So,' Leia continued, 'it's just the two of us then?'

'Us two and Kenobi,' Jan replied, huffing out a laugh. 'He really is our only hope.'

Leia's heart stopped abruptly, along with her feet.

'What?'

Her mum turned. 'Ben's back. Didn't Luke tell you?'

Leia shook her head. Her twin hadn't said a word.

'He flew in from Oz last week.'

'But—'

'His parents and Hazel are staying out there, but Ben says he's back for good.'

Every synapse in Leia's brain was in meltdown. This couldn't be true. It had to be a joke.

'He's really looking forward to seeing you again. Did you know it's been nearly ten years since they left?'

Leia gritted her teeth. She was well aware. A decade was not enough time to forgive Ben Walker. Her heart fluttered. And seemingly also not enough time to forget him.

She shook herself. 'Mum, even if Be— *he* is back, what's he doing here? Is he a waiter? Pot washer? Court jester?'

Her mother laughed. 'No, he's a chef.'

'A *what?*'

'Like us.' Her mother turned and continued down the corridor.

Leia jogged to catch up.

'You know,' her mother continued, 'he said me and your dad inspired him.'

'But he can't cook!' Leia spluttered.

'Course he can. It's what he's been doing for the last few years, just like you. I trust him.'

I don't.

'And besides, it's not like we have much choice right now.'

Leia looked from side to side, hoping to find a mirror hanging on one of the walls. She'd fantasised about meeting Ben Walker again. But in her dreams, she was poised and beautiful, the world at her feet, not make-up free and stressed out, her dreams crumbling around her.

'Mum, wait!' she hissed. The kitchen door was right ahead.

Her mother stopped. 'What, love?'

Leia ran a hand over her hair, checking the bun was still secure. 'I— I can't.'

'Can't what?'

She shook her head. Ben Walker was a bale full of last straws waiting to break her back.

'I know he and Luke used to tease you a bit—'

'A *bit?*'

'—but he's all grown up now. He's not a boy anymore, Leia, he's a ma—'

'Massive dickhead?'

'Leia!'

'Mum, he was bad enough back then. He'll be insufferable now. I can't work with him. I can't.'

Every muscle of her face tightened to hold back the tears. Of all days, this was the one she wanted to get through without crying. Ben would push every button, including those she'd buried ten years ago.

Her mother's eyes creased with concern. 'But love...'

Leia dug her nails into her palms.

'I'm sorry, Mum,' she whispered, her voice wobbling. 'It's him or—'

'Princess!'

Her gaze snapped to the flagstones beneath her feet.

'Kenobi!' her mother said, with the joy of someone beholding their saviour. 'Look who it is! Our beautiful Leia.'

'She is that,' a deep voice replied.

A shiver ran across her skin like wildfire, sucking out her breath. He sounded so... *different*. His voice was velvet, rich and dark, with a faint Aussie twang.

'Well, er,' her mother said. 'I'll leave you both to it. I'm just dashing to Castlemead Poultry and Tesco in Paulton to pick up a few more things. Text me if you think of anything else.'

In Leia's peripheral vision her mother untied her pinny.

'I'll take that, Mrs P.' Ben stepped forward.

Leia stared down at a pair of nonslip black chef's shoes and a pair of white trousers.

'Thanks, love. I'll be back as soon as I can.' She paused. 'Leia?'

She kept her eyes on the floor like a petulant teenager. 'Hmm?'

'Keno— Ben knows the new plan. He'll fill you in.'

She nodded in reply.

'Okay! See you both in a bit.'

The sound of her mother's footsteps echoed away.

Leia's roaring heartbeat filled the silence.

Ben cleared his throat and she tensed, trying to keep her balance as the floor seemed to tilt. His presence was overwhelming. It was like trying to stay upright in the face of a crashing wave.

'Princess?'

Then she was drenched with the realisation that nothing had changed. After ten long years he still used that stupid nickname.

'Don't,' she spat through gritted teeth. 'Don't call me that.'

He sighed. 'Leia Skye Perry. It's been a while.'

She grunted in response. Her neck was beginning to ache from eyeballing the floor for so long.

Another sigh. 'Are you going to look at me? I won't turn you to stone.'

Wanna bet? Your voice just turned my insides to lava…

'Please?'

As her head raised, so did her pulse. Her gaze travelled up his legs, his chef's trousers indecently tight around his solid thighs. His white jacket was short sleeved, his arms tanned and corded with muscle. Her journey stopped when she reached the indent at the base of his throat. She swallowed, her mouth suddenly dry.

Then, before she could stop it, her gaze pushed on through her fear and stubbornness to reach the top of Mount Walker.

Ohmygod.

Ben had been breathtakingly gorgeous at eighteen, with his messy dark hair, soulful brown eyes, soft long lashes and sinfully smart mouth. But he'd now grown into his looks. He was at least two inches taller, with broad shoulders that filled his chef's whites. His skin was tanned, with a faint regrowth of stubble. Ben Walker was no longer a teenage boy. He was all man, and so hot he was making her sweat.

His gaze caressed her face as if checking everything was where he'd remembered it was. Flames licked at the inside of her skin. He looked happy, but uncertain. His lips parted, the tip of his tongue darting out to wet them.

She squeezed her thighs together and suppressed a moan.

'Hey,' he breathed.

She opened her mouth but at the top of Mount Walker the air was too thin to breathe properly. All she managed was a gasp.

He smiled. The brightness of it was blinding.

She blinked.

'I've got a good feeling about this,' he said, his grin cheekier than a boxful of fresh peaches.

Leia crashed back to sea level.

'No. You are *not* going there,' she replied, pushing him out of the way. *Oh god, he's so... firm...*

She stomped into the large kitchen.

He followed. 'I find your lack of faith disturbing.'

'Seriously?' She took off her coat, wishing she was wearing anything other than her chef's whites underneath it.

'Uh-huh. People are counting on us. The gal—'

'No, Ben, the galaxy is most definitely not counting on us.' She faced him, keeping the large prep table in the centre of the room between them. 'The Foxbrookes are counting on us. And Mum.'

His smile was infectious. She took a step back before she caught it.

'We'll figure it out. We'll use the Force.'

She looked at the ceiling and let out a growl. 'That's not

how the—' She broke off and levelled her gaze at him. 'I'm not going to finish that sentence.'

He laughed, setting off butterflies in her stomach.

'Come on, Leia, you can do it. Repeat with me.' He lifted his hands as if about to conduct a choir. 'That's not how the Force works.'

She folded her arms across her chest to hold everything in. The laughter that fizzed inside her and was desperate to bubble out, the raw emotion at seeing him again, and the hot and heavy desire that ached between her legs.

'Do not draw me into your nonsense,' she said as primly as she could. 'We've got a job to do, and *apparently* you're a chef.'

He gave her a short bow. 'I'm not just *a* chef. I'm an *amazing* chef.'

She rolled her eyes. Despite the supermodel looks and body, he was exactly the same arrogant joker who loved playing pranks on her and pulling her pigtails.

Her hand unconsciously went to the nape of her neck. She still braided her long black hair, but now secured the plait in a tight bun. Ben Walker wouldn't be pulling anything again in a hurry.

'So, tell me where you've worked. What's your experience?'

He placed his hand on his chest. 'You don't trust me?'

'I don't know you.'

'Princess!'

'Don't.' She jabbed the air. 'Come on, out with it. I need to know what you can handle.'

He raised an eyebrow and her underwear ignited.

'I'll have you know...' He lowered his voice. 'I've served hundreds of diners a night, heading up the kitchens for a multinational corporation. *And* I've been awarded "employee of the year" for the last five years running.'

Holy shit. Maybe he could cook after all.

She cleared her throat. 'And would I have heard of this company?'

He shrugged. 'They're Scottish in origin.'

Hilton? Hyatt? Radisson? No, they didn't sound Scottish.

She didn't have time for this. 'What's their name?'

'McDonald's,' he replied.

'Aargh!' she yelled. 'I hate you!'

He cracked up. 'I know.'

She growled at him through gritted teeth. 'And I can't believe you just got me to say a line from *Star Wars*. I take it back. I don't hate you.'

He pouted. 'Don't say that, I wanted to tell you to let go of your hate.'

She gave up and hung her head. 'We're doomed.'

'Doomed?' came a voice.

She whipped around to face the second door into the kitchen as Leo Foxbrooke entered.

'It can't be that bad, surely?' he asked.

Leo was the third son of the Duke of Somerset. Blond, blue-eyed, handsome, and a year and a half younger than Leia.

She crossed the room and gave him a hug. 'Happy birthday, Leo. I promise tonight will go okay.'

He disengaged with a smile and shrugged. 'It's only a meal. It's Dad who's got his knickers in a twist about it.' He looked over her shoulder at Ben and frowned. 'Where's Perr— your mum?'

'She's just dashed out to get more supplies. Her order didn't turn up.' Leia gestured towards Ben. 'This is, er—'

Ben strode forward, his arm extended. 'Ben Walker. You probably don't remember me; I was a couple of years ahead of you at school. Best mates with Luke.'

Leo's eyebrows raised in recognition. 'Yes! I remember. You

had the whole *Star Wars* thing going on. You were Han Solo and Luke was... Well—'

'Jar Jar Binks,' said Ben, nodding. 'He was blessed with the looks *and* the voice.'

Leo snorted with laughter. 'Do you still have the costumes?'

'Yep, and I've got a stormtrooper outfit now as well.'

'No way! How much did that set you back?'

'Six grand.'

Leo whistled.

'Australian dollars. It's about three and a half sterling.'

'Is that where you've been living? I can hear a slight accent.'

He nodded. 'For the last ten years.'

'And you're a chef?'

'Yeah, I did a three-year apprenticeship at a restaurant in Sydney and gained my level three qualification in commercial cooking and patisserie. I've been head chef at Monimo for the past three years and we won the Chef Hat award for the past two.'

'Well played, man, congratulations. Are you back on holiday?'

Ben hesitated before replying. 'No, I'm back for good.'

Leo pulled a face. 'You chose Foxbrooke over Bondi Beach? Are you mental?'

Ben's eyes flicked to Leia's, then away. He shrugged and smiled at Leo. 'My heart's here.'

Leia's was currently hammering so fast she was sure it was audible in another galaxy.

'Perryyyyy,' whined a voice from outside. 'I'm hungreee.'

The door banged open and the youngest Foxbrooke sibling entered. Summer was blonde-haired and blue-eyed like her older brother, stunningly beautiful, and well aware of the effect she had on people. The baby of the family, she usually got whatever she wanted.

'Oh.' She stopped dead, surveying the room. Her eyes came to rest on Ben and didn't move.

She batted her eyelashes. 'I'm hungry,' she repeated, this time sultry, not whiny.

Jealousy roared in the pit of Leia's stomach. *No way, Summer. Not him.* She stepped forward as Ben took a step back.

'Mum's just popped out but I can rustle you up something quickly,' she said. 'How about an omelette?'

Summer frowned. 'Why are you here? Isn't today the opening of y—'

'Summer, right?' Ben interrupted, inserting himself between them.

Leia bit the inside of her cheek as she stared at the expanse of his back. She wanted to rest her head against it and weep.

'Things are going to get a bit busy in here,' he continued. 'Can I get you a plate of cold cuts and pastries for you to take elsewhere?'

'Summer, you can get food from the other kitchen,' Leo huffed. 'Let's get out of their hair.'

'What are *you* doing here then?' Summer replied, the whine back in her voice.

'One, to tell them twenty-three people just cancelled because they're sick,' her brother replied. 'And two, to see if they could use a hand.'

His exasperated tone gave Leia strength and she stepped out from behind Ben.

'Leo, it's your birthday. We've got this. You go and have fun.'

He frowned. 'You sure?'

'Yes. Positive.'

He smiled. 'Thanks, I appreciate it.'

'Me too,' Summer added, looking at Ben.

Ben's eyes stayed on Leo.

'And Estelle's riding over from the livery stables in a bit to set the dining room up,' Leo said. 'So that's one less job to do.'

'Thanks, Leo.'

He stepped forward and gave her another hug. 'Thank *you*,' he said before whispering in her ear. 'I'm sorry about everything.'

She nodded and squeezed him back.

'So...' Summer began.

Leo pulled back from Leia and rolled his eyes. He turned and grabbed his sister's hand.

'Oi! I haven't got my pastries,' she grumbled.

'Come on, squirt,' Leo replied, dragging her towards the door. 'It's my birthday, so you have to do what I say.'

The door closed behind them, leaving a weighty silence. Why had Ben really come home? What had made him drop the life he'd built in Australia?

She looked at his profile as he gazed at the kitchen door. What was he thinking? She stared at his lips, remembering the feel of them against her own. The memories scorched across her skin. That moment, in the sweet summer darkness of the garden, had been the highest point of her life. Right up until it imploded to create a crater in her heart that she didn't think would ever be filled.

She swallowed. 'Ben?'

A muscle twitched in his jaw. He took a breath and turned to her, his face a mask.

'Okay, we're down by twenty-three covers which buys us a bit of breathing room,' he said amiably. 'Let me run through your mum's plan and we can get started.'

❧ 2 ❧

'Your mum prepped the crème brûlées and the chocolate fondants yesterday,' Ben began. 'We just need to do the sugar toppings and chuck the fondants in the ovens fifteen minutes before they're ready for dessert. Luckily the birthday cake was made last week, so we don't need to make that, but I would like to make an ice cream.'

'What about the other courses?' Leia replied. 'Mum said she was going to Castlemead Poultry?'

'Yeah. The duke wanted individually cooked steak, but with only the three of us, that's out the window, so we're going for trays of Moroccan-spiced chicken and veg with preserved lemons. We can plonk them on the table and they can help themselves.'

'I remember Mum preserving the lemons last year. We can also raid the herb garden.'

He nodded. 'I know your mum made the brûlées and fondants before she knew tonight would go tits up, but a mint ice cream might suit a Moroccan theme?'

She nodded. 'I can make a meze plate to start with flat-breads, dips, kofte and some stuffed peppers with rose harissa. Mum always has a few jars of that in the larder. We've got plenty for the gluten-free crowd. How many vegetarians? Any vegans?'

'Three veggies. Your mum thought we could make them a chickpea tagine with chermoula?'

She looked at her watch, then crosschecked it with the clock on the wall. 'Do you want to make the ice cream first, then prep the trays for the chicken for when Mum gets back with them? I'll ring her now in case we need her to pick up anything else, then start with the dough for the batbouts. Okay?'

She's so fucking cool. He grinned. 'Yes, Chef.'

She pressed her lips together as if trying not to smile. Her eyes had been so sad a few moments ago, but now they were sparkling. He wanted to keep them that way.

He cleared his throat. 'If I may be so bold, Chef...'

She raised her eyebrows. 'Ye-es?'

'I've got a good feeling about this.'

She closed her eyes, but the corners of her mouth were twitching up. 'I hope you know what you're doing.'

He gave a silent fist pump at the *Star Wars* quote.

'Yeah, me too,' he replied, deliriously happy.

She opened her eyes. 'Did you just do your happy dance?'

'No, Chef.'

'Hmm.' She turned away and pulled out a drawer.

'In the interests of full disclosure, I fist pumped.'

She turned back and threw a cap at him. 'Put this on. You're still a scruffy-looking nerf herder.'

'Not stuck-up and half-witted as well?'

She smiled. 'I'm giving you the benefit of the doubt. You've got half an hour to prove you've changed.'

He wanted to say so much, but she was only just beginning to thaw. He didn't want to risk pushing his luck.

'Yes, Chef.' He put the cap over his unruly hair and shook his hips.

'What *are* you doing?'

'It's my happy dance.'

'Do I need to call an ambulance? Are you having a seizure?'

He threw in a few moves he knew she'd never seen him do before.

She slapped a hand over her mouth as she laughed. 'You're worse than Dad after he's had a few.'

'Your dad's my Jedi Master. Taught me everything I know.' He turned sideways to do the running man move. 'I am one with the Force and the Force is with me. I am one with the Force and the Force is with me.'

She shook her head, but her face was alight. 'I'm going to ring Mum. Get on with the ice cream.'

He stopped his dance and saluted. 'Yes, Chef.'

He watched her leave the room, still shaking her head. He couldn't remember the last time he'd felt so good. Sure, he'd been over the moon to land the head chef position at Monimo, and ecstatic when he picked up the Chef Hat awards. But that happiness was more of a relief after all the hard graft. It didn't feel like this. Right now, he felt lighter than a soufflé.

He pulled out ingredients to start the custard for the ice cream. He could have done a cheat version with beaten egg whites, but he wanted this to be the best. He wasn't just preparing a dessert for a birthday meal; he was proving himself to the woman who'd had his heart since the age of fourteen.

Whisking the sugar and egg yolks together, he smiled to himself. Back in Sydney he was in charge of a packed commercial kitchen and his word was law. Here, in the quiet kitchen at Foxbrooke Manor, in the depths of rural Somerset, he was taking orders, not giving them and it felt better than winning any award.

Growing up, he always knew Leia Perry was amazing. But he was an awkward, geeky teenage boy and she was his best friend's twin sister. So he followed Luke's lead and was an annoying little shit around her. Until the opportunity presented itself to make his feelings real.

He put the mixing bowl to one side and frowned. That had been simultaneously the best and worst decision of his life.

'Kenobi!' Jan entered the kitchen, laden with bags.

He rushed forward. 'Let me help with them.'

'Thanks, love, I'll grab the rest. There isn't much. Leia told me the ideas you both had over the phone. They're spot-on.'

She glanced at the mixing bowl. 'You're not making the ice cream from scratch, are you?'

'I want it to be perfect.'

She put her hand on his shoulder. 'Stay on target, Red Leader. We've got an industrial-sized ice cream maker in one of the back rooms. Use that.'

'I did tell him,' Leia called over from the other side of the room.

'I wanted it to be perfect,' he grumbled.

'It'll be perfect enough, love,' Jan said. 'You can show off to us another time.'

Would there be another time? He glanced over at Leia and she quickly looked away. She was so beautiful. His fingers itched to undo her bun, free her thick black hair and run his fingers through it.

'Kenobi!' Jan clicked her fingers in his face. 'Stay on target.'

OVER THE NEXT COUPLE OF HOURS BEN BUCKLED DOWN. Working in a kitchen was always a dance. With small spaces and lots going on, you had to anticipate someone else's actions or serious accidents could occur. Some people were thick, selfish, lazy or all three. Once he'd made head chef, he was able to weed those people out. Creating a proper team was what had really won the awards.

Here, working alongside Jan and Leia, he had the same feeling of synchronicity. As he lifted something out of the oven, Leia would lean over and shut the door. As Jan looked up for another utensil, he would hand it to her. They worked seamlessly as if performing a culinary ballet.

But even though he focussed on the job at hand, his awareness was always with Leia. He'd always looked up to her, but he was awed by the woman she'd become. Should he have come back sooner? Was he too late?

'Hey, Kenobi.'

He glanced up. Leia was sauntering towards him, a blowtorch in her hand.

'Let me guess.' He grinned. 'Ancient weapons are no match for a good blaster at your side?'

'Yep. Want to help me nuke some sugar?'

'Are we doing okay for time?'

She nodded.

'We're actually ahead of schedule,' Jan called over. 'Pretty much everything is in hand. Steve and Luke are coming over after work to help with the clear up afterwards. You two crack on with the brûlées. I'm going to check on the dining room with Estelle.'

She left and Leia pulled out trays from the fridge containing the ramekins of egg custard that had been chilling since the previous day.

'Can you line them up on one of the work surfaces?' she asked. 'I'm going to get the spray bottle and sugar.'

When she returned to the kitchen, she held the sugar she'd

selected behind her back.

'Okay, award-winning head chef,' she began.

'*Multi*-award-winning.'

'Okay, multi-award-winning, stuck-up, head nerf herder, how *exactly* would you go about this?'

He grinned. 'Sprinkle into each ramekin one and a half teaspoons of demerara because it's got a richer taste, give them a shake and a bang to settle the sugar, lightly spray the top with water, then use the blowtorch.'

'Humph.'

'Did I pass the test?'

She took a packet of demerara sugar from behind her back and put it on the counter. 'Maybe.'

'Can I be the one to use the blowtorch?'

She clutched it to her chest. 'No way, flyboy. That's my job.'

His heart rate rose. How far could he push his luck?

'Fair enough.' He shrugged as if he didn't care. 'So, just to make sure we're on the same page...'

'Yes?'

'I'll give them a shake and a bang, get them wet, and then you'll blow them?'

He kept his face poker straight as he watched the heat rise in hers.

'Is that the right order?' he asked. 'Or can I get them wet before I give them a shake and a bang?'

She opened her mouth but no words came out.

'Whaddya think, Princess?'

She raised the blowtorch and switched it on.

He took a step back.

'I think, Ben Walker,' she said, advancing on him, 'that you haven't changed one bit. You're still an utter scoundrel and only fit for Bantha fodder!'

Even though the blowtorch was perilously close to his

chest, he didn't think he could feel any better.

'So, you think a princess and a guy like me...?' he asked, raising an eyebrow.

'I'd rather kiss a Wookiee!' she hissed.

The door to the kitchen banged open and Jan entered.

'Leia, what are you doing?' she cried. 'Never point that at anyone!'

She turned it off. 'I was just showing him how to use it.'

'He's a professional chef, love. I think he knows his way around a blowtorch.'

Leia huffed. 'That's what they all say... Anyway, how's the dining room looking?'

Ben measured sugar into the ramekins as he listened to their exchange.

'Great. Estelle's done a fantastic job, as ever.'

'Is the whole family going to be there?'

Jan paused and frowned. 'Everyone except Henry.'

Ben remembered Henry Foxbrooke. He was the heir to the estate but had distanced himself from his hippie parents and lived in London.

'Is he ever going to come back?' Leia asked.

'He'll have to this summer,' Jan replied. 'It's his and Estelle's thirtieth and their grandmother's eightieth. They've got the biggest long weekend of parties planned. He can't get out of that one.' Jan looked over to him. 'Kenobi, are you going to be around this summer?'

He nodded.

'Fancy another job? Five days?'

'Love to.'

'Mum.' Leia's voice was low. 'You don't know if he's going to stick around.'

'I'm sticking around, Princess,' he called over. 'Now I'm back, I'm not going anywhere.'

❧ 3 ❧

'So far, so good,' Jan said as they re-entered the kitchen. The meze selection for the first course had been well received and the three of them had just finished delivering the trays of Moroccan lemon chicken and chickpea tagines.

Leia checked her hair was still neat as Ben took off his chef's hat and ran his hands through his thick locks.

'I'm only letting you take that off because we're washing up,' she said to him.

He smiled and her heart skipped a beat. '*Letting* me?'

Her mother cleared her throat. 'This is my kitchen, Leia, and I am not a committee.'

Ben fist pumped at yet another *Star Wars* quote and Leia rolled her eyes.

'Kenobi's got a beautiful head of hair. It always looks like he's just stepped out of a salon,' her mother said.

'Scruffy-looking nerf herder,' Leia muttered as she lifted up a tray of dirty dishes.

'Put that down, love,' her mother said. 'I need you two to

go to the cellar and pick up some dessert wine.' She scribbled on a scrap of paper and handed it to Leia. 'These are the ones I want. Don't worry if it takes a while to find. It's a bit of a mess down there. I've got it under control here and your dad and brother will be along soon to help.'

They took off their aprons and Leia led Ben through the rabbit warren of the ground floor corridors until they came to a narrow flight of steps leading to a scratched wooden door with peeling paint. She gave it a pull but it didn't budge.

'Do you need a hand?'

She gripped harder. After all the knocks she'd had over the last few months, she would not be beaten by this. 'No, I don't need any help.'

'You sure?'

'Yes,' she spat through gritted teeth as she tried to wrench it open.

'Clear your mind, Leia.'

'Don't you—'

'Use the Force.'

With a noise that was half grunt and half growl, she tugged hard and the door opened. The momentum sent her barrelling back into the brick wall that was Ben.

She felt his heat, his shallow breaths against her ear, the rapid thudding of her heart.

'I've got you,' he whispered.

Every nerve inside her was shorting out as desire crackled through her.

'You okay?' he asked.

Her nod was erratic.

'You're trembling.'

The Han Solo quote snapped her out of the moment. This was just a game to him. It wasn't real.

She shrugged him off. 'I'm not trembling and I'm not re-enacting a bloody movie, either.'

She flicked the ancient light switch just inside the door and stomped down the stone steps into the darkness.

He followed. 'Leia, I wasn't thinking about *Star Wars* just now. I promise.'

She ignored him, walking further into the cellar and squinting at the dusty bottles on the racks.

'Leia, please.'

In the furthest room was a long wooden table on which sat plastic bottle carriers. She grabbed one and brandished it at him.

'I don't need your help. I can use these. Go help Mum with the dishes.'

There was a loud bang from the other end of the cellar.

He turned his head. 'Was that the door?'

'I don't know and right now I don't care.' She sighed. 'I just want to find this wine, get out of here and go home.'

She turned her back to him, inspecting the dusty labels. The Foxbrookes may have lived in a stately home, but behind the scenes it was chaos.

'I'm just going to make sure it wasn't the door,' he said.

She shrugged and waited for him to leave.

As his footsteps receded, she let out another breath and rubbed her eyes. She was so tired of everything.

The light above her flickered, then went out with a sharp crack, entombing her in thick blackness.

'Ben!' she cried out. 'Ben!'

'I'm coming!' he yelled from the other room. 'Hang on!'

Over the sound of her own panicked breathing, she heard crashes as he felt his way towards her.

'I'm here!' she yelled. She hated the dark. There was something oppressive and terrifying about not being able to see where she was.

'Keep talking. It'll help me find you more easily.'

'I'm here,' she repeated, holding out her arms. 'Ben, I'm— Aarrgghh!'

'It's me! I've got you.'

She clung to him, too afraid to be away from his warmth and security.

His arms folded around her and he stroked her back. 'It's okay.'

'I'm s-sorry,' she said, her teeth chattering. 'I'm really scared of the dark.'

He held her tighter. 'I know.'

The rhythmic thud, thud, thud of his heartbeat against her ear soothed her.

'How?'

He let out a huff that whispered across the top of her head. 'We've been friends since we were seven. I've picked up a few bits of information about you over the years.'

'To use against me?'

He paused. 'I'm sorry.'

'Which particular incident are you sorry for? There's a bloody long list.'

'I know. Luke and I were twats to you a lot of the time. Can I make a blanket apology for everything I ever did to piss you off?'

She smiled against his chest. 'That's such a cop-out.'

'I agree. But I promise I'll make it up to you. Can I start by making you dinner next week?'

She stiffened. Thoughts and questions raced through her mind. What should she read into that?

She swallowed. 'Why did you come back?'

His silence was as suffocating as the darkness.

'From Australia,' she continued.

He didn't respond.

'Ben?'

He took a breath. 'I was offered my own restaurant.'

She raised her head to look at him, even though there was nothing to see in the blackness. 'What?'

'After the second award, an investor approached me. She's a big name in the industry and fully or partially owns several restaurants in Sydney. I'd been saving to open my own place anyway so had money put aside, just not enough. She offered to invest and provide project management for development of the site.'

'Oh my god, Ben. That sounds incredible!'

'It was.'

'So, are you doing it?'

'No.'

'Why not?'

She could feel the tension in his body as he hesitated.

'Ben?'

'It's complicated.'

Was it about a woman? *Does he have a girlfriend?* The thought ran like ice down her spine.

'Tell me.' She tried to keep the quake of fear out of her voice.

He shifted his body, putting his hands on the outside of her arms as if he could look directly at her. She stared up, imagining the expressions on his face as he began speaking.

'When I went to Oz with my family, it was a clean slate. I could be whoever I wanted. And I—' He broke off and sighed. 'I also wanted to prove myself. To show... that I could be good at something and make a success of my life. So, I did. But when this opportunity arose, I realised there would be no going back. I would be fully committing to a life in Australia.'

He paused, his thumbs moving hypnotically up and down her inner arms.

'I didn't have a girlfriend— I *don't* have a girlfriend, and my apartment was rented. Apart from my job, a few friends, Mum, Dad and Hazel, I didn't have anything keeping me in Sydney.'

'Your family, friends and job sounds like a lot to keep you there?'

'Maybe. But Hazel and my folks have their own lives. And I have friends here, too.'

'But why choose Somerset over Sydney?'

'I missed—' He cleared his throat. 'I missed Foxbrooke. Oz was amazing, but was more like an extended holiday. The UK always felt like my home. It's where my heart is.'

Leia's was trying to punch its way out of her chest.

'What are your plans?'

His thumbs stopped moving.

'I mean, now you're back,' she continued.

He paused and took a big breath. 'I've already signed on with a few temp agencies. I'll get a job and take it from there.'

'But what if it's not as good as you remembered here? What if you get bored?'

His fingers were now moving restlessly up and down her arms, trailing goosebumps in their wake.

'It's better than I remembered,' he said softly. 'And I'll never get bored.'

Silence stretched out in the darkness.

'Leia?'

'Yes?'

'That night, I—'

'Don't.'

He squeezed her arms. 'Leia, please?'

She shook her head even though he couldn't see. She didn't want to revisit the humiliation of her brother and his other friends leaping out from the bushes as she kissed Ben for the first time, crowing to each other as to who won what in their bet.

'Leia, I'd wanted to kiss you since I was fourteen. But I was an insecure, idiotic teenage boy and you were Luke's sister. The bet was my excuse to do what I'd been dreaming about for four years.'

'But—'

'I tried to explain but you were so angry and I knew I'd blown it. I wasn't sure if I was going to go to Australia with my parents. But after that night I made up my mind.'

She thought back to what she'd said to him a decade ago. All her hurt spitting out like venom.

'I was horrible to you,' she said quietly. 'I'm so sorry, Ben.'

'Don't be. I had every opportunity to play it differently. Taking that bet was the coward's way out. I was trying to get what I wanted with you and still save face with my mates.'

'So, you *wanted* to kiss me that night?'

She heard a soft chuckle. 'I wanted to kiss you every day since the end of year nine.'

'But you were such a...'

He tugged her body flush with his. 'Scoundrel?'

Oh my god. 'Ye-es,' she stammered. 'You *literally* pulled my pigtails.'

She felt his fingers exploring the bun at the nape of her neck, then he released the hairband holding the braid in place and it tumbled like a rope down her back. He wrapped his hand around it and his lips grazed her ear.

'I know,' he whispered. 'It's what boys do to girls they really, really like.'

'I don't understand,' she murmured, every cell in her body lighting up with longing.

He placed a soft kiss below her ear. 'It's very simple.'

She clung to the rock of his shoulders, hanging on for dear life as all the blood left her head and rushed south. 'It is?'

He nibbled her neck and she shuddered. 'Yes, Princess.'

'Don't—'

'I call you princess,' he continued as he trailed kisses across her skin. 'Not because I'm trying to be funny or a dick. It's because to me, you always have been, and always will be, a princess. You're beautiful, clever, creative and funny. You're incredible, Leia.'

Tears stung her eyes. It had been years since she'd thought any of those things about herself. She'd allowed herself to be smart and hardworking, but that was as far as it went.

'Is this some kind of sick joke?' she asked, her voice cracking.

'No! God, no, Leia.' He cupped her face with his hands, resting his forehead on hers. 'You don't believe me?'

She hesitated. She wanted to believe him, but recent events had shaken her trust in men to the core.

'Leia...'

His lips were so close. She was frantic to kiss him, but she wasn't going to close the gap if this wasn't real.

'Yes?'

'I'm not going to move,' he murmured. 'Put your hands wherever you want on me. Then you can see how much I want you.'

She could feel the thrum of tension in his hands, feel the unevenness of his breath against her mouth. Could she do this? Could she explore his body the way she'd always dreamed?

'Do it, Leia. I'm all yours.'

The darkness made her bold. She had the chance to live out her fantasies, even if only for one night.

With trembling fingers, she followed the contours of his

shoulder muscles, along his arms to the hot skin of his forearms. She placed her hands atop his as they cradled her face.

'Lower,' he said.

She swallowed, then reached forward until her fingertips touched his chest. She could feel the rise and fall of his rib cage as if he was struggling to breathe. If this was an act, then he deserved an Oscar.

'Lower.'

She traced her fingertips down his chest. Was she really doing this? Could she do it? A million tiny voices joined together inside her to chorus 'yes!' She'd been starved of any touch like this for so long. Why shouldn't she take what he was offering?

Before she could throw any more barriers in her own way, she ran her hands across the front of his trousers.

Holy mother of god.

She sucked in a breath as she gripped around his solid length. Ben Walker was big and broad *everywhere*.

A nervous giggle escaped her.

'Is something funny?' he whispered, his breath ragged. 'Because I'm in agony.'

'Is that a lightsaber in your pocket, Ben, or are you pleased to see me?'

He threw his head back and laughed. 'God, Leia, I... I fucking lo—'

She reached up to grab his face and brought his lips crashing to hers.

They may have been in darkness, but a thousand fireworks detonated at once inside her, filling her head with light and her body with flashes of desire.

He tugged her closer, one hand twisting around her braid, the other grabbing her backside and pulling her against his cock.

The kiss in the garden ten years ago had rocked her world. This one was obliterating it. As his tongue slicked against hers, she was sure she would die with pleasure. She'd often wondered if she'd imagined how good his lips felt, if she'd unfairly compared other men to him and found them lacking. Now she knew with soul-searing certainty that no-one could ever make her feel the way he did.

She ground her pelvis against him, seeking the delicious friction that would send her into oblivion. He lifted her and she clasped her legs around his hips, rocking into him, her tongue dancing with his as he moved. He sat her down on the edge of the table, sweeping the plastic bottle carrier to the floor with a crash.

He tore his mouth from hers, kissing and sucking down her neck. 'Leia, Leia, god, Leia.'

Sensation sparked in bolts of light along her limbs, out through the tips of her fingers and toes. Every part of her was electric, every cell fizzing as it overloaded.

She was in a crackling, uncontrollable storm of pleasure, almost painful in its intensity. It was as if the thunder had been rumbling for the last ten years and had now built to earth-shattering proportions.

She tugged the buttons of her jacket open, desperate to release the pressure, then pulled her vest top and T-shirt bra up over her breasts.

'Fuck, Leia!'

She cried out into the darkness as his mouth found her nipple, pleasure spiking to her clit as he sucked it deep. She squeezed her thighs together, chasing her release.

Then his mouth was gone and he lifted her to her feet.

'Turn around,' he growled, spinning her so her back was against his front, the ridge of his cock rubbing against her bottom. 'Kiss me.'

She turned her head and his lips were there, ready to devour her. He held her to him, one hand rubbing the tip of her nipple, the other unzipping her trousers and reaching under the waistband of her pants.

He broke the kiss as his fingers found her wet centre. 'Oh god, Leia. You're... You're so... Fuck!'

'Kiss me,' she gasped.

He did, imprisoning her between his lips, tongue, and fingers as he drew circles of fire over her clit.

She was shaking now, surrendering herself completely to his mercy as the wind whipped tighter and tighter around her. He held her close, chasing her into the raging storm. Deep inside, lightning was fighting to find a way out, crackling against the inside of her skin.

She broke the kiss and cried out again. It was too much. She was going to break apart.

'Leia, my Leia, my Leia.'

My Leia. His words were the tipping point, the moment the energy was released and the climax torn from her body.

She screamed his name as the shockwave thundered through her, shaking and shuddering in his arms as wave upon wave of blinding pleasure overwhelmed every one of her senses.

'My Leia, my Leia,' he whispered as his fingers eked out every drop of feeling from her orgasm until she was limp and empty in his arms.

Then he lifted her and sat back on the table, cradling her and peppering her face with kisses as if he couldn't stop.

She was floating through the infinite blackness of space, adrift in his arms. He'd turned her inside out and upside down and she couldn't remember who she was any more.

Shouting and banging echoed through the cellar towards them.

'Oh my god!' Reality crashed through her as she suddenly remembered exactly who she was, where she was, and what she was meant to be doing.

He placed her carefully back on the ground. 'It's okay, the door must have blown shut earlier. We've got time.'

Leia heard her name being called.

'Oh my god, Ben. It's Dad and Luke!' She redressed quickly, smoothing down her hair. 'Where's my hair band?' she hissed. 'I need it to secure my bun.'

She felt his hand as he gave it to her.

She twisted her hair back up. 'I can't see a thing.'

'Hold onto my hand. I'll lead you out.'

He guided her back through the cellar towards the voices.

'Leia? You down there?' her father called out.

'Yes,' she yelled back. 'With Ben, but the lights have gone out.'

'The bloody door's jammed again,' shouted her father. 'But don't worry. The Force runs strong in our family.'

She groaned and Ben chuckled.

'Stand back!'

There was an almighty thud.

The door didn't move.

'Nice try, old man,' Leia heard her brother say. 'Let me at it.'

There was a louder thud. The door rattled in its frame but it still didn't budge.

'Dad! Luke!'

'Yeah?'

'Were you pushing the door? It opens outwards.'

There was silence on the other side.

Ben snorted.

Two seconds later there was some more grunting and the door flew open to reveal her dad and brother on the other side.

'Not a bad bit of rescuing, huh?' her father said. 'You know, sometimes I amaze even myself.'

Leia shook her head. Her parents never let the opportunity to quote *Star Wars* pass them by.

'Thanks, Steve,' said Ben. 'Jan wanted us to get some dessert wine but the lights blew, so we're going to need a torch.'

Her dad held one up. 'She said the fuses were a bit temperamental and handed me this. I'll go get it. I know where it's stashed. You three go back and help clear up. I won't be long.'

He turned the torch on and went past them into the darkness of the cellar.

Leia turned for the kitchen, paranoid that her whites were covered in dusty handprints, or her messy hair was telling everyone exactly what she and Ben had just been doing.

'So, did Ben get it?' her brother asked.

'Get what?' she spluttered.

'The job at your restaurant,' he replied. 'I told him a couple of months ago that Tim did the dirty on you and now you've lost your business partner as well as your boyfriend.' He looked over his shoulder at Ben. 'The launch was meant to be tonight but nothing's happening until she can get staff. Did I tell you the bird Tim copped off with was their waitress?'

Leia stumbled, putting her hand on the ornate flock wallpaper as her head went dizzy. She stared at Ben. Underneath his tan he was white.

'Leia—' he began.

'You knew?' she whispered. Her gaze found her brother's face. 'And you *told* him?' she shouted.

'Am I missing something here?' Luke asked. 'What's the big deal?'

For months Ben had known about her humiliation. He'd

spent the whole night with her and never said a word. Why? Was it all just an attempt to butter her up before waltzing in and taking over her dream, just as she was recovering from it being trampled on by another deceitful man?

'I've got to go,' she said, her teeth chattering violently in her head. 'Tell Mum sorry and I'll speak to her tomorrow.'

'Lei,' her brother said, frowning. 'What's going on?'

'Leia—' Ben started, reaching for her.

'Don't!' she spat. 'I hate you.'

She turned and ran, but not before she heard his reply.

'I know.'

❅ 4 ❅

Leia ran away from the manor and down the high street, her footsteps a percussive *slap-slap-slap* that broke the night-time silence.

Foxbrooke was a small town, with streets so ancient and picturesque they were often used for filming period dramas. This late in the evening it was quiet and peaceful which was what Leia needed. She reached a glass-fronted shop, the windows papered up on the inside, a sign outside reading 'The Clear Palate – opening for business soon.'

Fumbling to unlock the door, she let herself in.

Inside, her eyes slowly adjusted to the darkness and the space. Tables and chairs were piled high in the middle of the room, covered by a dust sheet. At the back end was the kitchen, and a corridor that led to the toilets, utility rooms, a small office, then the rear of the building.

This had been her dream. To open her own restaurant. It had been *their* dream. Her and Tim. But somewhere along the line he'd fallen out of love with her and into the arms of her friend, Leanne.

'It's your fault. You never made time for me. You always put the business first. I've tried to make it work with you, but you make it too difficult. I need you to buy me out.'

Leia pulled a chair from the pile and sat down, staring at the whitewashed walls as memories continued to needle and taunt her.

'We can't have any colour on the walls and definitely no local artists exhibiting their crap. We're not a community café. The food should be the focus, not some tasteless painting some old git did.'

'You pretentious FUCK!'

She stood, pushing the chair back with a screech, and stalked towards the back of the building.

Flicking on the office light she went to a pile of boxes, rooting through them until she found the one she was looking for. She carried it back into the main room and turned on the lights.

Fuck Tim. She wasn't going to let him ruin this for her. She was going to make this place her own and that started tonight.

Inside the box were small tins of paint she'd bought to try out different colour schemes. They were unopened after Tim's pronouncement on the necessity of sticking with white. *'We're called The Clear Palate, Leia. Let's have all our messaging on-brand, okay?'*

She prised open the first lid. Inside was a golden sunny yellow. She held it in one hand, a small paintbrush in the other and faced the white wall.

Thoughts of Tim flooded through her like an overflowing storm drain, full of filth. She couldn't do this with his energy tainting her.

'Anger leads to hate, and hate leads to suffering,' she said out loud. 'The dark side are they. Once you start down the dark path, forever will it dominate your destiny.'

Her eyes fluttered closed.

'Remember, a Jedi's strength flows from the Force.'

She let out a long, slow breath.

'Let go of your anger. Let go of your hate.'

In her mind, she imagined standing beneath a waterfall of pure white light as it flowed into her body.

'I am one with the Force and the Force is with me.'

She opened her eyes.

'I am one with the Force and the Force is with me.'

She dipped the brush into the pot, lifted it, and flicked the paint at the wall. It splattered in an arc of golden drops, glistening in the light.

'I am one with the Force and the Force is with me,' she continued, dipping and flicking, dipping and flicking, her voice getting stronger and louder as the white walls came to life.

When the yellow paint pot was empty, she moved onto another, then another, until there was only one left.

'I am one with the Force and the Force is with me!' she roared as she flicked the last of the paint from the final pot.

She turned in a circle, exhilarated as she surveyed her handiwork. The walls were a riot of colour and excitement. This wouldn't be a place where people photographed their food, it would be a place where they enjoyed it and the company of the people they shared it with.

There was a knock at the door and she spun to face it.

'Yes?'

It opened and Ben entered. His eyebrows lifted as he looked from her to the walls and back.

She glanced down at her chef's whites, now rainbow splattered.

He cleared his throat. 'It looks amazing.'

'I am one with the Force and the Force is with me.'

He nodded.

They stared at each other in silence, her heart tumbling in

her chest from the rollercoaster of emotion she'd been on that night.

He looked wretched and uncertain, his broad shoulders hunched as if carrying the weight of the world on them.

'Can I come in?'

She shrugged, torn between wanting to run into his arms and kick him onto the street.

He took a step forward and she took one back.

'Look, Leia. I'm just going to lay it all out and you can do with it what you want. I'm going to get to the point and then fuck off and leave you alone.'

She crossed her arms in front of her.

He ran his hands through his hair. 'Okay, I admit that wasn't really getting to the point.'

She squared her shoulders, bracing herself for what was coming next.

He held her gaze without blinking. 'Leia, I love you. I've been in love with you since I was fourteen. I left for Oz because I blew it and wanted to make something of myself. I wanted to prove I was a better person than you thought I was.'

Every muscle in her body tightened.

'I stayed in touch with Luke, so I knew you were in a long-term relationship with Tim. When I won those awards, when I accepted them, the only person I thought of was you. I wanted to show you what I'd done. I wanted to make you proud. I didn't lie earlier. My heart's always been in Foxbrooke because you're my heart.'

Her eyes started to sting.

'When I was offered the chance of my own restaurant, I didn't want to take it because it felt like I would be finally closing the door on any chance of us. And when Luke told me what Tim had done, I didn't think twice about coming home.'

He let out a sigh.

'I didn't let on I knew what had happened to you because I could only imagine how difficult it must have been. I didn't want you to think I was the same twat who you knew from ten years ago. I wanted you to see I'd changed. I wanted you to trust me again.'

She bit the inside of her cheek to keep tears from spilling out.

'Leia, it's okay if you don't want to be with me. No matter what happens between us, I'm not leaving Foxbrooke. But I need you to know that I love you and I want to be with you. Working with you tonight...' He broke off and smiled, shaking his head. 'It was perfect. I'd love to work for you—'

'What? *Here?*' she choked out. 'When you've been in charge of a kitchen twenty times the size?'

He nodded. 'I left my ego behind in Oz. I just want to be happy. And I'm happy next to you.'

'You'd be fine not being the boss? Working *under* me?'

His eyes darkened. 'I'd do anything to be under you.'

Heat burned across her cheeks. 'But I could never afford you.'

He shrugged. 'I've got plenty of money saved up. If you offer me the job, I'll do it for minimum wage.'

She didn't know what to say. She could see how earnest his expression was and feel the truth of his words. They may not have seen each other for a decade, but before that she'd seen him almost every day for most of her life. Take away the childish pranks when they were growing up and she knew without question he was a good man.

The light seemed to dim in his eyes and he opened his palms as if to show he had nothing left to hide.

'I've said what I wanted to,' he said. 'Luke's got my number, so you can always reach me. You can ask me anything, interview me, chew me out, whatever. I'll be there.' He gave a rueful smile. 'This has been the best night of my life. Thank you, Leia.'

He turned to the door.

'Ben! Wait.'

He didn't move.

She crossed the room and took his hand, tugging him to face her.

His eyes were strained, his lips pressed together as if steeling himself for the final crushing blow.

'Ben, I—' she broke off, her mouth dry. All the feelings she'd bottled up for years about him were finally bubbling to the surface. He'd spoken his truth and now she would speak hers.

'Ben, I love you, too. I was so hurt back when we were kids because I loved you so deeply. After you left, I squashed those feelings down. But they never really went away. And now...' Heat bloomed inside her, burning her skin. 'They're even more powerful than before. I love you.'

He looked completely stunned. 'I... I *didn't* know.'

She smiled, feeling lighter than she had in years. 'Ben Walker. Yoda one for me.'

He lifted her up with a whoop.

She shrieked with laughter and threw her arms around his neck as he spun her around.

He stopped moving, leant down and brushed a kiss across her lips. 'Leia Perry, I love you so much. I've got a really good feeling about this.'

'And so have I,' she replied.

His lips found hers again and she let his kiss take her to another galaxy far, far away.

EPILOGUE

One year later

Ben gave the stainless steel surfaces a final wipe down. After a busy Saturday night in the kitchen of The Colour Palate, he should have been tired, but he was wired and on edge.

He glanced around the spotless kitchen. That night, he'd let his sous-chef go home as soon as the last table had been served. He needed to be alone to get his head in the right place.

From the dining room he could hear Leia cleaning up. No matter what time they finished, or how exhausted they were, they always left the restaurant spotless before walking home together. Working with her was easy; she felt like part of him.

He changed out of his chef whites, bundled them into a wash bag and went to find the love of his life.

'Hey,' he said, lounging in the doorway and admiring her. 'That was quick.'

She straightened, her eyes flicking over him and her cheeks

pinking. 'You look good enough to eat. Why didn't you just walk home in your whites?'

He shrugged, feigning nonchalance, whilst his tummy did a loop-the-loop. 'I dunno, maybe I wanted to show you I'm not a scruffy-looking nerf herder?'

'Nerf herders are the best,' she replied. 'I'm only with you for the nerf.'

He raised an eyebrow and advanced on her. 'Really?'

'Uh-huh, without my daily portion of nerf meat, I get cranky.'

He reached her side, his mouth at her ear. 'Would you like me to give you one now?'

Her breath quickened as she glanced at the large windows at the front of the restaurant. He grinned. She was actually considering it.

She pushed him back. 'Don't tempt me to the dark side.'

He laughed. 'What do you mean? I'm Ben Kenobi, not Ben Solo.'

'Scoundrel.'

He bowed. 'At your service, highness.'

She rolled her eyes, then hesitated.

'Ben...'

'Yes?' His stomach flip-flopped again. She had a look about her that made him uneasy.

'Can we sit down for a minute?'

'Sure.' He pulled out a couple of chairs, adrenaline spiking uncomfortably in his blood.

They sat opposite each other. Her hands twisted in her lap. This did not look good. He scanned back over the day, the last few weeks, months, the whole of the last year for something he might have missed.

'Is everything okay?'

She nodded. 'Yes, of course, it's more than okay. It's just... Well... I wanted to talk to you about something.'

Please let this be a good something. 'Go on.'

'This year,' she began, 'has been incredible. *You've* been incredible. You've never asked for anything. You've just turned up for me, each and every day.'

He shrugged. That was easy. It had been the best year of his life.

'And I feel awful—'

'About what?'

'That I haven't done this before. I want to offer you half of the business.'

His heart soared.

'I know we talked about it once,' she continued. 'And you said you wanted to invest. It would mean I could clear the loan I took to buy Tim out. This is your business as much as it is mine and I want us to be equal partners. In it together. I'm so sorry I haven't asked sooner.'

He shook his head and smiled. 'I totally understand. You needed to be sure about me. And yes, I'd love to. There's only one thing I want in this world more than to invest in your restaurant.'

Her brow creased in confusion.

This was it. He took the small box from the back pocket of his jeans.

I am one with the Force and the Force is with me.

He flipped the lid to show her the diamond ring and took a deep breath.

'Leia Skye Perry. You are the centre of my galaxy, the Force that keeps my heart beating. Will you marry me?'

He watched as her expression stopped still with shock, then lit up with happiness.

'Oh my god, Ben, yes! Yes! Yes! Yes!'

She leapt on him, covering him with kisses as he laughed with joy. He hauled her onto his lap and gently pushed the ring on her finger.

'So, whaddya think?' he asked. 'A princess and a guy like me?'

She nodded. 'It's the perfect happy ending. And...'

'Ye-es?'

'Much as I love my parents, I've never been fond of the surname Perry, so I'm going to take yours.'

His heart was going to burst. 'Leia Skye Walker. I like the sound of that.'

She rested her forehead on his. 'May the Force be with us.'

He brushed his lips across hers. 'Always.'

THE END!

II
LOVE AD LIB -
EXTENDED EPILOGUE

LOVE AD LIB - EXTENDED EPILOGUE

One year later

Libby tucked the skirts of her dress into her underwear. This was it. Third degree burns or good luck for the next year.

'You really don't have to do this, you know,' Henry said, his brow furrowed.

She jumped up and down on the spot, adrenaline shooting through every nerve. The short meadow grass had been baked soft by the summer sun and felt silky and warm under her bare feet, even at half eleven at night.

'It's all good,' she replied, rolling her shoulders and cracking her neck. 'I'm not wearing any artificial fibres, and I've been practising with hay bales.'

'Libby! Libby! Libby!' Henry's family were chanting her name by the bonfire, his father blowing a ram's horn.

'And besides,' she continued. 'You've just done it.'

'I've got over seven inches on you.'

She grinned. 'I love your seven inches. Can I have a play with it later?'

The worry lines on his face dissolved as he laughed. 'Absolutely.'

She stared at him, her heart overflowing. The past year with Henry in Somerset had been the happiest of her life.

'Libby! Libby! Libby!' A drum joined in the chanting.

'Okay!' she yelled. 'I'm almost ready.' She glanced at the bucket of river water that Henry was carrying. 'Don't even think about it.'

He nodded. 'I promise I won't use it unless you catch alight.'

She pointed two fingers between her eyes and his.

'You'd better not, Henry, or that seven inches of yours is going to be shortened with immediate effect.'

He gave her a salute. 'Yes, ma'am.'

'Count me down!' she called out to his family.

'Five! Four! Three! Two! One!'

'Incoming!' she yelled, sprinting towards the fire. The flames had died down since it was lit earlier that evening, but she could still feel the heat as she approached.

She leapt into the light, surrounded by the sound of whistles, whoops and musical instruments created from various animal parts. In her peripheral vision she could see Henry hovering with the bucket of water.

She landed, safe and exhilarated, on the other side. Henry abandoned his bucket, dropped to his knees and ran his hands up and down her legs.

'Get a room!' Estelle cried.

'I'm checking for sparks,' he replied.

'No shortage of sparks between those two,' guffawed their father.

Libby giggled and pulled Henry to his feet. 'I'm fine! And now we've got good luck for another year.'

He pulled her into his arms and held her tightly to his chest. She could feel the fast thudding of his heart.

'I'm fine,' she repeated, stroking his back. 'Happy Midsummer's Eve.'

His shoulders relaxed and he pulled back and gazed at her.

'It's nearly midnight. Fancy coming with me to look for a magic fern flower?'

'The lucky charm for lovers?'

He nodded.

'Has anyone, ever, in the history of the world found one?'

'*I* did.'

Her eyes widened. 'When?'

'Last year. When you were sleeping under the oak tree, I crept into the woods and found one. It gave me the luck I needed to win your heart.'

'Uh huh, so why didn't I get to see it then?'

'The magic only works if it's kept secret.'

'Okay...' She glanced around. She'd been getting used to the countryside at night, but outside the bright glow of the fire, everything seemed very, very dark.

'Can I sit this one out?'

His face fell.

This was odd. Henry was one of the most straight-down-the-line people she knew and the last person she could ever imagine wanting to look for a mythical plant.

'Is it important to you?' she asked.

He nodded, his face serious. 'I won't leave your side, and we don't have to go far.'

She squared her shoulders. If it was important to him, she was all in. 'Okay, let me grab my shoes and we can go and look.'

. . .

At the edge of the meadow, by the Foxbrooke river, was an ancient wood. Libby held Henry's hand tightly as they approached the ink-black trees.

Connor and Leo strolled towards them.

'Have you been looking for the magic fern, too?' she asked.

'Nah,' Leo replied. 'We needed a leak.'

'Fairies are abroad tonight,' Connor said. 'I needed to make sure Puck didn't change Leo from a metaphorical ass into an actual one.'

'Oi!' his brother retorted. 'I went with you because you're scared of the dark.'

Connor shrugged. 'That's true, but you're still the biggest ass in Foxbrooke.'

'Bollocks. I have the *finest* ass in Foxbrooke. There's a key semantic difference.'

'If the cap fits...'

Libby snorted with laughter. 'Well, we're looking for a magical fern flower.'

Connor patted Henry's shoulder. 'Good luck.'

As Connor and Leo ambled away, she turned to Henry.

'Weird...'

'What is?' he replied, leading her through the trees.

'They didn't take the piss that we're on a wild goose chase.'

'Hmm. They obviously have faith in our quest.'

She grinned at him, making out his smile in the darkness. 'Okay then, Sir Henry Fernfinder, lead on.'

He paused and looked around, as if trying to get his bearings. 'Erm... This way.'

She held his hand tightly as they went deeper into the wood. Apart from an owl hooting in the distance, all she could hear was their breathing, the swoosh of her skirts and the odd snap of a twig beneath her feet.

Up ahead, a tiny light was suspended about six feet off the ground.

She stopped dead. 'Henry!' she hissed. 'What's that?'

He shrugged. 'Firefly?'

'Do they have them here?'

'Dad's trying to breed them, so, maybe?'

He led her towards it.

'Henry! It's a fairy light! Up in the tree!'

He didn't seem fazed. 'Maybe Titania and Oberon are up to something?'

She pointed. 'Look! There's another one. Over there.'

Now her eyes had fully adjusted to the darkness, she could see a trail of fairy lights.

'Henry, did you do this?'

He shook his head.

'Do you know what's going on?'

'Do you want to follow them?'

Her heart beat faster in her chest. He hadn't answered her last question. Did he know what this was about? Is this what Connor and Leo were really doing here?

Excitement propelled her forward on the trail, dragging Henry with her. She slowed as they reached a cluster of lights close to the ground.

On the forest floor was a large fern, surrounded by fairy lights, and in the middle of the foliage was a bouquet of tiny white flowers on long stalks.

'Henry! It's the magic fern flower!'

He smiled. 'They're Libertia grandiflora, also known as Liberty flowers.'

She threw her arms around his neck and kissed him, her heart stuttering with happiness.

'Henry, you're the sweetest, kindest, most thoughtful man in the world. This is such a wonderful surprise. I love it!'

The lights lit up his smile. 'Go pick your flowers. It's almost midnight.'

She pressed another quick kiss to his lips, then disengaged and reached down. The bouquet was tied together with a silk ribbon and the white petals seemed to glow in the darkness.

'Oh, Henry, they're so—'

She stopped abruptly. He was on one knee before her, holding out a ring.

'Liberty Fletcher. You're my magical fern flower, my lucky charm and the love of my life. You've made me the happiest man in the world, and I want to be with you, always. Please, would you consider marrying me?'

Every cell in her body was stunned into silence, then burst with joy.

'Oh my god! Yes! Yes, yes, yes, yes, yes!' She dragged him to his feet, clutching the sides of his face and covering it with kisses. 'I love you, Henry. I love you so much.'

'I love you too, Libby,' he grinned. 'Do you want to see the ring?'

'Do owls hoot in the woods?'

On cue, there was a hoot in the distance and they both laughed.

She looked at the ring as he held it up in the half light.

'The stones have been in the family for generations,' he said. 'I got the jeweller in the village to reset them. It's gold, because you're the sunshine in my life, with a ruby in the centre to match your hair. And it's surrounded by diamonds because, apparently, they're a girl's best friend.'

Her words and her breath stuck in her throat.

'Is it okay? Do you like it?'

'I- I don't think I've ever seen anything so b-beautiful,' she stammered. 'Oh my god, Henry. It's just so...'

He gently pushed it onto her ring finger. 'Perfect.'

The owl hooted again, as if to confirm his words, and she blinked away her happy tears.

'So now we've found the magical fern flower, is the quest over?'

He reached down and lifted her into his arms.

'Lovely Libby,' he said, resting his forehead against hers. 'It's only just beginning.'

THE END!

❧ III ☙

AN UNHOLY AFFAIR - EXTENDED EPILOGUE

AN UNHOLY AFFAIR - EXTENDED EPILOGUE

Monaco - six months later

The sky was a cloudless, azure blue. The sun warmed the pale-yellow sand and sparkled across the surface of the sea to the horizon.

It was a perfect day and Jack had a perfect view—that of his pregnant wife on a sun lounger under a parasol, reading a book.

He was currently experiencing levels of contentment designed to cause spontaneous singing, or the hugging of strangers. Jack often wondered if God—with whom his relationship was still rather nebulous—or the universe, held a balance sheet of everyone's happiness quota for their life. And as unconditional love had been in rather short supply during his childhood, he was getting a surfeit of it now.

Eveline glanced up from her book and smiled at him. 'So then, what's my surprise?'

'It can wait. I don't want to take you away from a particularly exciting bit of the story.'

She peered at him over the top of her sunglasses. 'Jack Newton, are you teasing me?'

He grinned. 'What's that one called again? *Cold-War Double-Agent Zombie-Nazis at Mince Pie Cottages on the Cornish Cove?*'

Eveline giggled. 'Almost exactly. Only minus the cold war, double agents, and zombie Nazis.'

Sitting on the sun lounger next to her, Jack rested his hand on her leg. Touching Eveline didn't need to be sexual, but it felt necessary. It completed a circuit, grounded him and made him whole.

'Who's my current rival?'

'Well, husband, you've got some stiff opposition in this one.'

He raised an eyebrow. 'I bet he's not as stiff as me.'

Eveline glanced around, furtively. 'Jack!'

'What? I'm English. We're renowned for our stiff upper-lips.'

She smirked. 'You delight in being naughty.'

Leaning forward, he kissed her. 'As do you, wife...'

Her cheeks turned pink, and she fanned her face with the book. 'Well, the hero of this book is a secret Duke, who's set up a service delivering cupcakes by penny farthing bicycles.'

Jack snorted, and she frowned at him.

'Sorry,' he said, passing his hand over his face to try and remove the laughter. 'Go on...'

'But he's gone up against our heroine's business. *Her* company delivers cupcakes by tricycles.'

Jack couldn't hold it together any longer, laughing so hard, a few people glanced their way.

'It's *very* romantic,' Eveline hissed at him.

'What are their names?'

'I'm not going to tell you. You'll only laugh.'

'Don't you like making me happy?'

He loved how hard she was trying not to smile.

'And don't forget,' he continued, running his hand a little higher up her thigh. 'I need to have the intel on my love rivals so I can... *Outperform* them...'

Her breathing hitched. 'You... Er...'

He reached the bottom of her swimsuit and hooked a finger underneath the material.

'Jack!' She batted his hand away with the book. 'We're in public!'

He shrugged, loving how flustered she was. 'It's the south of France. Half the people on this beach are topless.' He raised an eyebrow. 'Want to join them?'

'You're absolutely incorrigible.'

'And you love it...'

Energy sparked between them, and his cock jumped. When he was with Eveline, Jack was convinced telepathy was real. The more time they spent together, the closer they became, and the more effortlessly they seemed to read each other's minds.

Eveline broke first, fanning her cheeks again. 'When can I get my surprise?'

'You can have it on one condition.'

'And what might that be?'

'Tell me the names of the main characters in your book.'

She huffed. 'Okay, but your surprise had better be worth it.'

He grinned and nodded. 'You'll love it.'

Eveline sat up and crossed her legs, facing him. 'The leading lady is called Wren Butterscotch and her hero is Heath Wyld.'

He pressed his lips together tightly to stop a snort from escaping.

'Happy?' she asked.

'Ecstatic,' he replied, reaching into the canvas tote at his feet and pulling out a paper bag.

'Ooh! Is it food?'

'Yes. I bought you some pig's ears.'

She frowned. 'Really?'

'They're also called "elephant ears", "palm leaves", "French hearts", "shoe-soles", and even "glasses".'

'Now I'm intrigued...'

Jack passed her the bag. 'Palmiers. These ones are ham and cheese.'

Eveline pulled out the pastries. 'They smell amazing!'

Biting into one, her eyes fluttered as she chewed.

'You like?' he asked.

She swallowed. 'They're the best pig's ears I've ever had.' She held the bag out and he took one.

They sat, gazing happily at each other as they ate. Then Eveline leaned forward and kissed him.

'Thank you. They were absolutely delicious.'

Jack smiled. 'My pleasure. How are you feeling?'

'Perfect.'

'The baby?'

She took his hand and placed it on her swollen belly. His heart jumped as he felt movement.

'Is that...?'

She nodded. 'He likes pig's ears too.'

His throat was too full of emotion to speak.

She placed her hand over his.

'I...' he began.

'I love you too,' she replied.

Eveline suddenly felt too far away. Jack hauled her onto his lap so he could hold her closer.

'That's better,' he murmured.

She let out a happy sigh. 'I love it here.'

'We could stay a bit longer?'

'Maybe a couple more days?'

'Or months?'

She glanced at him. 'You know we can't. It's Robert and Shirley's wedding in a couple of weeks and you're the best man.'

He smiled and kissed her. 'I can't wait. Then there's the official opening of the church hall to look forward to.'

'The music and arts festival,' she continued.

'And the summer fete. I expect you to win big.'

She grinned. 'My money's on you to come first in the "cake baked by a gentleman" category.'

'Aren't men allowed to enter the rest of the competition?'

'Of course they are, but the ladies who run it are so old they assume men will never win, so have created that category to give them a chance at a prize.'

Jack laughed. 'That's hilarious. I feel like entering everything now.'

Eveline prodded him. 'Don't you dare. You're good enough to rival me.'

'High praise indeed,' he murmured, brushing another kiss across her lips.

'It's going to be a very busy summer...'

He stroked her stomach. 'And then in September, this little one will make his appearance.'

She nodded, her face shining. 'I can't wait.'

His heart was overflowing with love. 'Me neither. It's going to be amazing.'

Eveline smiled. 'I'm so glad we've been able to take this break. It's helped give me space to breathe.'

'I hope it's shown you that even Super-Vicar needs some time off?'

She nodded. 'Yes, but you've already done that. Meeting

you has given me perspective. I can't help everyone if I run myself into the ground.'

He kissed the top of her head. 'Exactly.'

'You've changed my life, Jack.'

He smiled. 'Not as much as you've changed mine.'

Holding her tightly to him, Jack gazed out at the sparkling sea. With Eveline at his side, happiness was as limitless as the horizon.

THE END!

IV
THE UPPER CRUSH - EXTENDED EPILOGUE

THE UPPER CRUSH -
EXTENDED EPILOGUE

Poland - the following year

Come on, you can do this!

Lifting her bow, Estelle gave Duke a nudge and let out a war cry.

He took off, and she braced her thighs around him as he galloped down the sandy track.

The first target was already in range. Letting the arrow fly, she quickly grabbed another, not allowing herself the luxury of seeing if she'd hit the first mark or not.

She kept firing until Duke reached the end of the run and came to a walk, breathing heavily. Leaning down, she patted his neck. 'Top job, partner.'

Glancing back up the track she tried to work out how well she'd done, then turned Duke and trotted back to where the spectators were.

James came forward to meet her. 'Fantastic run. That's definitely put you in the top ten.'

She leapt off Duke's back. 'I'm so glad we brought him with us instead of hiring a horse here.'

James pulled her into his arms and kissed her. 'Definitely. And I've enjoyed the road trip. Now I can tell everyone I've been to hell and back.'

She giggled. 'It's called *Piekło*.'

'Which translates as hell. Can we visit Koniec Świata on our way home?'

'Which one's that? "Bad Meat" or "Monsterville"?'

'It translates as "the end of the world".'

'Would that make you happy?'

'Extremely. I bloody love Poland.'

'Then we'll do it.'

'How long have you got until your next run?'

'Half an hour?'

'Okay, can you meet me in the practice field afterwards, fully tooled up?'

Huh? 'Is there something you want me to hit?'

'Maybe.'

'For the love of god, will you stop asking me to shoot an apple on the top of your head? It's so fucking dangerous and I'm never going to do it.'

He grinned. 'But I trust you.'

'Jesus Christ, James, I don't trust me.'

He dropped a kiss on her forehead. 'Don't worry. It's not that.'

'Then what is it then?'

'You'll see...'

EXHILARATED AFTER HER SECOND RUN, ESTELLE CANTERED up to the practice field where James was waiting. Huge balloons had been tied to the front of each target.

'What's this?'

'You start at that end,' James said, 'and I'll meet you at the other. I want to see if you can burst all of them.'

'O-kay... That's pretty easy.'

He shrugged, a strange expression on his face. He looked... *nervous?*

Wheeling Duke around, she trotted to the end of the run and checked her quiver. As long as she didn't miss, she had enough arrows left to hit all of them.

She urged Duke into a canter. 'Let's do this.'

Letting the first arrow fly, she followed its progress as it burst the balloon. The word 'Will' was taped to the target behind.

Huh?

Firing the second arrow, she revealed the word 'you'.

Oh, my god.

Heart racing, she burst the third balloon to see the word 'marry' behind it.

Her hands were trembling, but she managed to clip the edge of the fourth balloon and it burst, revealing the word 'me?'

She slowed Duke as they approached the end of the run. James was waiting next to the last two targets left. One had a green balloon stuck to it, the other a red one.

'What's it to be, Star? Will you marry me?'

Lifting her bow, she shot the green balloon, showing the word 'YES' behind it. As the balloon burst, something dropped out of it.

James strode forward, picked a small box from the ground and brought it back to her.

'Estelle Gloria Elizabeth Foxbrooke,' he began, flipping the lid to reveal an enormous diamond ring inside. 'I believe this belongs to you.'

Her mind was spinning. Even though she knew they'd get married at some point, this gesture had side-swiped her.

'What's behind the red balloon?' she asked, her throat dry.

He raised an eyebrow. 'Are you really going to go there?'

Lifting her bow, she let the last arrow fly.

The balloon popped, revealing the words 'ALSO YES'.

Throwing back her head, she laughed.

'Well? Are you going to put me out of my misery?'

Dismounting, Estelle fell into his arms. 'Yes, yes, and also yes,' she said, peppering his face with kisses. 'It was never going to be any other answer.'

'Thank fuck for that,' he rumbled. 'Now, please, can you try the ring on? Your mom said it was the right size.'

'My *mom* knows you were going to do this?'

'I think everyone knows by now. I told your dad and Henry that I was going to propose, and ran the ring past your mom and mammy for their approval.'

She gazed at it. The diamonds had been cut to create a star. 'It's so beautiful.'

'For the most beautiful woman in the universe.' He eased the ring onto her finger.

'It's a perfect fit.'

'Just like us,' he replied, lowering his lips to hers.

Estelle opened to him, pouring her soul into their kiss, her body flooded with love. In James, she'd found her perfect match. He challenged, excited and loved her like no other, and she was looking forward to spending the rest of her life challenging, exciting, and loving him right back.

THE END!

V
THE LOVE POSITION - EXTENDED EPILOGUE

THE LOVE POSITION - EXTENDED EPILOGUE

One year later

Eyes closed, Sophia breathed slowly in and out, her mind flowing through the sensations in and around her.

Her arms were on the side of the natural pool, a towel to cushion them, her head resting to one side. The rest of her body floated behind her, gently rising and falling in the water as she inhaled and exhaled.

It had been another glorious June, the midsummer sun heating the water and burnishing the grass till it was silky soft. Sophia spent as much of her time outside as she could, barefoot, breathing in the flower-scented air and grounding to the energy of mother earth.

Her lips curled into a smile. Her brother joked that she'd turned into a hippy, but Isaac said she was a living goddess. And as for her? She was just following her own body's intuition and doing what felt right. And at this moment, she wanted to be in water.

At the sound of the house door opening, she lazily opened her eyes to see Isaac. He raised a hand in greeting as he made his way towards her, and a thrill of excitement tingled in her tummy.

Reaching the edge of the pool, he lay down so his face was level with hers and smiled.

'How are you doing, my sweet and beautiful wife?'

'I need a kiss.'

Leaning forward, he brushed his lips against hers, sending sparkles across her skin.

'Have you been in here for the last two-and-a-bit hours?' he murmured.

Sophia nodded, kissing him again. Over the last few months, her sex drive had gone through the roof, and Isaac made sure he checked in with her after every yoga class in case his services were required.

He drew back, concern clouding his features. 'You aren't cold?'

'Not today.' She gave him a dreamy smile. '*Definitely* not today.'

Isaac's face froze for a second, then he swallowed. 'Do I need to call anyone?'

Sophia shook her head. 'Not yet. It's likely to be hours before we need to.'

'What can I do?'

'Help stimulate my oxytocin...'

Eyes lighting up, he jumped to his feet, flinging his clothes to the ground.

Sophia giggled. Their hypnobirthing teacher had told them that nipple stimulation and orgasms were good for easing and speeding up labour, and Isaac had been one hundred per cent onboard with this advice.

Slipping into the water, he came behind her, his hands finding her breasts.

She let out a low moan as he rubbed the end of her nipples. 'That feels so goooood...'

Isaac nipped her neck, the heat of his chest firm against her back as he braced his feet on the bottom of the pool.

Desire pulsing through her, she angled her head over her shoulder to kiss him again. As his tongue tangled with hers, electricity arced between her lips, nipples and clit, sparking through her body. Every part of her was swollen and primed for release.

Her belly had been tightening for hours but she hadn't told Isaac. She didn't want him to worry when he was teaching, and the sensations felt natural and normal even though she'd never experienced them before.

But now, as one of his hands moved between her legs, the contractions were becoming stronger. Just like when she'd had tantric experiences, now too, her mind and body seemed to merge with the invisible currents of energy around her.

What might have felt like period pain, was wrapped up in pleasure, two colours complementing each other and joining into a swirling rainbow of light as it moved between her and Isaac, the water, the air, the earth.

The orgasm came suddenly, rocking through her. Ecstatic pleasure underpinned by a shuddering power that seemed to split her apart.

Her breath rushed in and out like a spring tide, following the feelings as they swelled and crashed inside her.

'You okay, love?'

Sophia nodded, lost in the sensations. 'More. More...'

Isaac's fingers circled, rubbed, tweaked as if they were her own, knowing when to ease back and when to push forward.

Climax after climax rolled through her, a never-ending

rollercoaster of pleasure that kept expanding the boundaries of her awareness until her edges dissolved into the universe. Every supercharged particle pulsing like a star.

A tiny part of her still knew where she was and what was happening. That part checked in with her intuition. Sophia had spent so much of her life doubting herself and second-guessing every decision, but since being with Isaac, her innate confidence in who she was and what she wanted kept growing.

And when she became pregnant, it was like a switch had been flipped, grounding her so completely in her own body that all she needed to do was ask what was right, and the answer came to her, as solid as the ground beneath her and as clear as the skies above.

Now, letting go of any fear and trusting the messages from her body, she surrendered to the process, tumbling through the tightening, the opening, the pressure. The sharp pleasure and ecstatic pain.

And through it all, Sophia knew she wasn't alone. Isaac held her, helped her, breathed with her. His calm strength kept some part of her grounded as the rest of her hurtled through the universe on an unstoppable journey.

Time passed, but it was fluid, not quantifiable.

Then there was a lull, a moment of perfect stillness, as if the world was holding its breath.

'Transition?' Isaac murmured in her ear.

Her breath quietening, she nodded. 'I think so.'

'Do you want to get out of the pool?'

Sophia asked herself the same question.

The answer came back, louder than a bell, and she shook her head. 'I'm okay. Everything's okay.'

As she said the words, she felt the change inside her, the distant rumblings of a storm on the horizon as her body went from opening to releasing.

Sucking in a breath as the contraction hit, she exhaled slowly, bringing her feet to the bottom of the pool.

Isaac held her through it, kissing her neck as she subsided again into peaceful stillness.

'Just tell me when,' he said softly. 'Okay, love?'

Sophia nodded, gearing up to ride another great wave as it bore down through her body.

There was a stinging sensation as her baby's head crowned.

'Breathe... Breathe, love,' Isaac whispered.

She did, drawing on all her reserves to get her up the final slope of the mountain.

Four more powerful contractions thundered through her.

'Isaac, the head's out,' she gasped.

He moved behind her as she felt the baby turn, marvelling at the instinctive act that required no thought or input from her.

Another wave built.

This was it.

'I'm here, love. I'm ready,' came Isaac's sure voice behind her as she sucked in a breath, then exhaled in a rush as her baby slipped out.

'Reach down,' Isaac said.

Pushing away from the side of the pool, Sophia put her hands into the water, taking her baby from Isaac as he passed it through her legs.

Holding the child in her arms, she gazed at the little face as it opened its eyes, staring at her as if it already knew her soul.

'Hello, little one,' she said softly. 'Welcome to the world.'

The baby's mouth opened, and it gave a cry. Then its head moved, its lips smacking, as if wanting food.

Carefully supporting the head, Sophia moved the baby to her nipple. It latched on immediately, prompting another contraction.

'Oh!'

'You okay?'

She nodded, unable to tear her gaze away from the sight of her child suckling at her breast. 'Just another contraction. It's a good thing.'

Time seemed to stop as the three of them were held in an embrace so profound, Sophia knew it would alter them forever. Love flooded through her, deeper than the ocean and wider than the sky. She would always be her own person, but she was now connected to the baby in her arms and the man cradling them both, on a level that went beyond the physical and emotional to a plane so vast it was beyond comprehension.

'Shall we see what we've got?' Isaac asked.

A laugh escaped. 'Yes! I can't believe I didn't think of that.'

He kissed her cheek. 'Girl or boy, it doesn't matter. They're already perfect. Just like you.'

As he moved the umbilical cord out of the way, Sophia glanced down.

'It's a girl,' Isaac said, his voice full of wonder.

Sophia's eyes filled with happy tears and more laughter bubbled out. 'A little girl!'

Isaac tore his gaze from their baby to her, his own emotion spilling down his cheeks.

'You're a warrior, a goddess, and a queen, Sophia. I didn't think it was possible to love you more, but I do. You're my everything.'

She kissed him. 'And now we're three.'

He nodded, appearing lost for words.

As their baby suckled, another powerful contraction rippled through her and she felt the placenta release. For the first time in hours, she glanced around. The sun had almost set, and the light was beginning to fade.

Sophia giggled. 'Thank god the pool is spring fed. How long will it take to be clean again?'

Isaac grinned. 'Not long, although I don't think anyone else should swim in it for a few days. Should I ring the midwife? Get her to come over?'

'In a bit. Right now, I just feel like getting into bed and snuggling.'

'With a big mug of hot chocolate?'

She nodded. 'Sounds perfect.'

TWO HOURS LATER, THE MIDWIFE HAD BEEN AND GONE AND Sophia was in bed, her daughter sleeping peacefully in her arms.

Isaac entered the room, holding his phone. He swiped at the screen, then pocketed it.

'Aeroplane mode is on and my parents send their love.'

Sitting on the end of the bed, he rested his hand on her leg. 'And they're relieved we didn't call her "something weird and hippy".'

Sophia snorted with laughter. 'Linden and Maya aren't exactly common names.'

Isaac grinned. 'Yes, but I've been priming them for months to expect something along the lines of "Lentil Moonbeam", so anything other than that they were going to accept with open arms.'

'A very cunning plan, Mr Hayward.'

'One of my better ones, for sure. Did your mum like her name?'

Sophia nodded. 'Although, to be honest, I couldn't really tell. She spent most of the call screaming with excitement and crying.'

Isaac's smile was full of love. 'Imagine what she'll be like tomorrow when she meets Linden for the first time.'

'It's going to be amazing. Although prepare yourself for my dad to take off one of his gold chains and present it to her as if she's the second coming.'

Isaac chuckled. 'Her first bit of bling.' He squeezed Sophia's leg. 'Can I get you anything?'

She yawned and shook her head. 'Just you.'

Getting up, he turned off the main light, then got into bed beside her.

Sophia settled into the crook of his arm and let out a happy sigh. 'If I fall asleep, will you take her?'

'Of course.' Isaac kissed the top of her head. 'Rest, love. I'm here if you need anything.'

Closing her eyes, she let herself sink into his embrace, Linden snoozing on her chest.

Warmth filled Sophia's heart. She was exactly where she wanted to be and everything was right in her world. Letting herself drift into sleep, one word and one feeling suffused her very being: love.

THE END!

VI
CHRISTMAS OFF SCRIPT - EXTENDED EPILOGUE

CHRISTMAS OFF SCRIPT - EXTENDED EPILOGUE

Christmas Day - one year later

'Do you need to use your set square?' Leo asked his eldest brother as Henry adjusted the tiny posy of evergreens pinned to the front of Leo's suit for the third time. 'Maybe your spirit level?'

'It was on the wonk,' Henry replied patiently. 'Ella's an artist. She'll notice details like these.'

'No, she won't. She's too in love with me for that. All she's going to see when she walks down the aisle is the best-looking Foxbrooke.'

'Not just the one with the best-developed ego?' Connor asked with a grin from his position at the window overlooking the manor's gardens.

'No, that's Dad,' Leo replied cheerfully. 'I'm the best-looking.'

'Wasn't Henry on the cover of *Vogue* magazine?' Connor continued.

'Seriously? Why does everyone keep going on about that?' Leo asked. 'It was bloody years ago!'

'Actually—' Henry began.

'Anyway,' Leo interrupted. 'My day, my glory. Your job is to make sure we're on time at the church, hand over the rings, then make some heartfelt speeches at the reception about how amazing I am.'

Connor's laugh was warm. 'I think we can do that.'

Leo smiled, his contentment sprinkled with impatient excitement at seeing Ella again. The past year with her had been the happiest of his life. She was his favourite person to be with, think about or talk about. His colleagues at work had been amused and bemused by his levels of adoration, however his family had not. They knew better than anyone else the importance of Ella in his life. Whether when they were children, or now as adults, endlessly in love with each other.

'I can't believe it snowed,' Connor said. 'I should have put a bet on it.'

'The Christmas gods are on our side,' Leo replied. 'I just wish it was enough for us to travel back from the church in a one-horse open sleigh.'

Henry raised his eyebrows. 'For a couple of hundred metres walk?'

'Yes! It would make it more festive.'

'And a health and safety nightmare. We're not prepared for that amount of snow in the UK.'

'There's a sleigh at the back of the old carriage house.'

'Which is rusty and rotted because the last time it was used was hundreds of years ago for a jaunt around the park.'

Connor grinned. 'Could you be any more obsessed with turning your wedding into a Hallmark movie?'

'Oh yes,' Leo replied happily. 'I want us to change our surname to Christmas.'

'What?' Arthur exclaimed as he entered the room. 'Renounce the good name of Foxbrooke?'

Leo smirked. 'The British press and most of the general public think our name is anything *but* good.'

'Bugger them,' Arthur retorted. 'Bunch of bally fools. Why d'you care what *they* think?'

'I don't. But you have to admit, being Mr and Mrs Christmas would be amazing.'

'No, it wouldn't. And what would be next, eh? Calling your offspring Holly and Ivy?'

'Those are brilliant names for twins!' Leo turned to Henry. 'There we go. Next year, when Libby gives birth, you can call your kids that. Or Robin and Noel if they're boys.'

Henry shook his head. 'Not going to happen.'

'Okay, then I'll suggest it to Estelle. She's due to pop her two out around the same time, isn't she?'

Connor laughed. 'Can I be there when you suggest it to her?'

Leo pulled a face. 'Maybe I'll send a text.'

'Leo, m'boy,' Arthur said, a frown on his face, 'You're not serious about this name-changing nonsense, are you?'

'Fear not,' Leo replied. 'For mighty dread has seized your troubled mind. Glad tidings of great joy I bring to you and all mankind.'

'What?'

'I'd quite happily change our surname to Christmas, but Ella wants to be a Foxbrooke. Can't think why.'

Arthur's eyes turned glassy. 'Because she's a poppet and an angel,' he replied gruffly. 'And we're bally lucky to have her.'

A silence settled on the room and Leo's throat tightened. They *were* lucky to have her. And he was the luckiest of them all.

Connor slung an arm around his shoulder and squeezed. 'Time to go. You've got a wedding to get to.'

⚜

'It's too light,' Michelle said as Willow applied Ella's make-up. 'You can't tell she's wearing any.'

The brush stilled and Ella held her breath.

'We're going for a natural look,' Willow replied with a smile.

Put it on thicker, then blend it.' Michelle leaned in. 'Ells, love, I wish you'd just let me do it for you.'

'Michelle!' Summer swooped in with the power of the midsummer sun. 'Why don't we do a quick live together? Obviously no shots of Ella, but we can show off our outfits and tease for the big reveal later. What do you think?'

There was a stunned beat, then Michelle straightened as if she'd received an electric shock. 'Yeah! Yeah, let's do it now!'

Ella squeezed her lips tightly together to stop a laugh escaping as Michelle hurried after Summer from the room. A year ago, her stepmother realised she had more to gain from being kind to Ella than cruel. Not only did it win her the approval of her husband, but it gave her access to Summer and her millions of followers. So far, Summer had resisted any collaboration with Michelle, but now she seemed ready to take one for the team and buy Ella some breathing space.

'I never imagined this,' Ella murmured to Willow.

'Marrying my brother?' she replied quietly. 'Or Michelle being nice to you?'

Ella glanced at the room reflected in the mirror. Vivienne and Dervla were chatting to her birth mother, and Lila was talking animatedly to Billie-Mai and a heavily pregnant Kyla-Marie. It was a sight she'd never believed could happen.

'Everything,' Ella said. 'I keep thinking I'm going to wake up and find it's all been a dream.'

Willow smirked. 'But instead you're going to wake up each morning next to my brother. I'd call that a nightmare.'

Ella giggled. 'That's the best bit. He's—' She sighed happily. 'Perfect.'

'And so are you. Happy with what I've done?'

'Yes, thank you. I feel like a princess.'

'You're more beautiful than that.' Willow placed a diamond tiara on Ella's head. 'You're a queen.'

Ella blinked at her reflection. 'I can't believe Gram-Gram let me wear this.'

'It's the ultimate sign of her approval. And it looks incredible on you. I tried to place a bet with my family that Leo would cry when he sees you for the first time. But they all agreed he's going to lose it.'

'I think *I'm* going to cry when I see *him*.'

'That's why I used waterproof make-up. I've prepared for all eventualities.'

There was a knock at the door, and Dervla went to let Ronnie into the room.

Ella caught her father's eye in the mirror, the love and pride in his expression making her tear up. Willow pulled her chair back and Ella stood, making her way to his side.

Ronnie took her hands. 'My little girl.' His voice cracked. 'All grown up.'

'You ready to give me away?'

He shook his head. 'I feel like I've only just got you back.'

Ella threw her arms around him. 'I'm not going anywhere, Dad. You've got me for life.'

He held her tightly and drew in a ragged breath. 'God bless you, love. God bless.'

'Willow,' Billie-Mai called out. 'You owe me a tenner. Told you my dad would be the first to cry.'

Ella pulled back from her father, and they both grinned at each other.

'I can't help it, love,' Ronnie said to Billie-Mai. 'Just look at her.'

'I know, Dad. But you can't set her off or the make-up will be ruined.'

'It's waterproof,' Ella said.

'Thank f—god for that,' Billie-Mai replied. 'And isn't it time for us to go?'

'I'll get the photographer,' Vivienne said. 'A few naturalistic photos, then we'll get you into the car.'

'Are you sure?' Ella asked. 'I can walk?'

Vivienne raised an impeccably shaped brow. 'In couture? In the snow? No, honey.'

Ella grinned. 'I can wear my Converse?'

Her future mother-in-law placed the back of her hand on her forehead and shuddered theatrically. 'Heathen!'

Dervla chuckled. 'You sound just like Gram-Gram, Vivi.'

'Dear lord,' Vivienne said as everyone laughed. 'I take everything back. You can wear rainboots for all I care.'

Michelle re-entered the room with Summer, and Ella glanced her way. 'You ready to go to the church, Michelle? I think the cars are outside.'

'Yes, doll. All good. And you look lovely, by the way.' She turned to her husband. 'Don't she look pretty, Ron?'

'She does, love.' Ronnie sidled up and took her arm. 'Just like you.'

Even under the layers of make-up, Ella could see her stepmother blushing.

The photographer entered and gave them all a wide smile. 'I'm just going to get a few quick shots, then we'll head to the church. Can I have the bride and bridesmaids by the window, please?'

Ella went over and stood between Billie-Mai and Lila on one side, and Summer and Willow on the other. She'd also asked Kyla-Marie, Estelle, and Libby if they wanted to be bridesmaids, but all three were heavily pregnant and had graciously declined.

'Gorgeous,' the photographer said. 'Now I just want to ask if any of you know what Cinderella said when her photos didn't show up?'

Summer pulled a face. 'Huh?'

'Some day my prints will come!' she replied with a grin, snapping photos as everyone cracked up. 'Did you hear about the two cell phones that got married?' she continued. 'I heard the reception was excellent.'

Lila snorted. 'I can't believe I'm laughing at these!'

Ella giggled. 'I know!'

'What do you call two spiders that just got married?'

'Newly-webs!' Ella cried, and everyone cheered.

The jokes kept coming, easing the nervous tension in the room, and when they left for the church, Ella was bubbling over with happiness.

However, standing just outside Saint Saviour's church, holding her father's arm, Ella's heart beat faster. Inside was Leo, waiting for her. *Her!* She wanted to run towards him.

'You ready?' Eveline asked with a smile, her cassock almost hiding her baby bump.

'Yes!'

'Okay, I'll go in now. When you hear the music change, you're up!'

Ella nodded, then smoothed her free hand over the silk satin of her dress. It was a simple design, the fabric of the skirts pinned up in layers, giving the effect of snow drifts all the way to the floor. On her feet were a pair of jewelled heels, patterned with crystals that Willow and Summer had stuck on. They were beautiful, but Ella wasn't used to walking in them and was worried about catching her heel in the metal grating over the vents in the church floor.

'I've got you, love,' her father said gruffly. 'I won't let you fall.'

A lump of emotion filled Ella's throat. 'Thanks, Dad,' she whispered.

The music changed, and she took a deep breath. This was it. Stepping forward with her father through the stone arch, Ella was only vaguely aware of the brightly-dressed people and the greenery inside the church. Her eyes sought out one person, and one person alone: Leo.

Her heart skipped a beat as her eyes locked with his. He was jaw-droppingly handsome in his suit, his blond hair shining and his aquamarine eyes lit up.

Leo. Leo. My Leo...

Emotion flooded through her, overflowing down her smiling cheeks. As they approached, tears tracked down Leo's face and her father sniffed loudly next to her. And by the time Ella reached the altar and her dad placed her hand in Leo's, she wanted to bawl with happiness.

Eveline stood in front of them behind a small lectern. As the music stopped, she ceremoniously placed a large box of tissues on it, causing everyone in the church to laugh.

'Happiness is expressed in many forms,' she said. 'And I had a feeling that this ceremony would warrant a family-sized box of tissues. It reflects the amount of joy and love we all feel as we witness the joining of Ella and Leo in holy matrimony...'

THE CEREMONY SEEMED TO PASS IN THE BLINK OF AN EYE. Ella's hand only left Leo's when they signed the register and when she placed the wedding band on his finger. The rest of the time, he held her hand tightly and spoke his marriage vows as if intending for the whole of Foxbrooke to hear them. Then, when Eveline declared them man and wife, he kissed her with such passion and adoration that her head spun and her knees buckled. Everyone cheered, clapped, and wolf-whistled. Then the organ started up, and the bells began to ring.

Leo lifted his lips from hers. 'I love you,' he said. 'Thank you for making me the happiest man in the universe.'

'I love you, too,' she replied. 'More than anything.'

He grinned. 'Even more than Christmas?'

She nodded. 'Yes. Believe it or not, such a thing is possible.'

'You're my wife. That proves *anything* is possible.'

Linking his arm with hers, they started back down the aisle together as husband and wife. Ella let her gaze travel over the crowd. Seeing her work friends, Leo's, his extended family. She caught Zach's eye, and he whooped loudly, his genuine happiness for her making her heart even lighter.

Nearly at the door, the heel of one of her shoes caught in the grating, and she stumbled with a gasp.

Leo held her upright. 'You okay?'

'One of my shoes just came off.'

Dropping to his knees, he lifted the bottom of her dress and fished around until he found it. Then he knelt before her and held it up. 'Cinderella?'

She giggled.

'Shall we see if the slipper fits?'

Leaning on his shoulders for support, Ella lifted her foot and Leo eased the shoe back on.

'A perfect fit!' he cried.

'Thank you, my prince.'

He got to his feet and gazed at her. 'My princess,' he murmured, then leant down to brush a kiss across her lips. 'Ready for the fairytale ending?'

'I am.'

With the snow falling like white confetti, Ella took Leo's arm, and they stepped out into a winter wonderland. The weather may have been cold, but her heart was warm, knowing that this Christmas, and every Christmas to come, Leo would always be by her side. He was her best friend, her husband, and her perfect happily ever after.

THE END!

Thank you for reading Foxbrooke Extras! Have you checked out the Kinloch series yet? Laugh-out-loud steamy romcom that's heating up the Scottish Highlands!

Start with the multi-award-winning Highland Games!

You can get all of my books in print, audio, or eBook format, as well as special offers, early releases, and exclusive deals at **www.eviealexanderbooks.com**

REVIEW FOXBROOKE EXTRAS!
WRITE A REVIEW & MAKE MY DAY!

Thank you so much for reading Foxbrooke Extras! I hope you enjoyed reading this collection as much as I enjoyed writing it!

Even if just a few lines (or star rating), writing a review is the most amazing thing you can do! It helps people find my books, and lets them know what you loved about them.

You can review Foxbrooke Extras at:
Apple
Amazon
Bookbub
Goodreads
Kobo
Barnes & Noble
Google Play
And any other storefront or platform you use!

And, if you want to share more about Foxbrooke Extras on

NEWSLETTER SIGN-UP

In my newsletter you get Evie news before anyone else, as well as exclusive content and goodies.

Newsletter subscribers are my extra special friends, and get everything from bonus epilogues, 19,000 words of deleted sex scenes from Highland and Hollywood Games, free stories, free audiobooks, extracts from my current work-in-progress, and exclusive offers and giveaways.

Sign up now!

www.eviealexanderauthor.com/subscribe/

ALSO BY EVIE ALEXANDER

Get all of Evie's books in print, audio, or eBook format, as well as special offers, early releases, and exclusive deals at www.eviealexanderbooks.com

THE KINLOCH SERIES

HIGHLAND GAMES

Zoe's given up everything for a ramshackle cabin in Scotland. She wants a new life, but her scorching hot neighbour wants her out. As their worlds collide, will Rory succeed in destroying her dream? Or has he finally met his match? Let the games begin...

Tropes

Small Town, Enemies-to-Lovers, Grumpy/Sunshine, Fish-out-of-Water, Opposites Attract, Forced Proximity

HOLLYWOOD GAMES

In a last-ditch attempt to save Kinloch castle, new lovers Rory and Zoe throw open the doors to a Hollywood superstar. But when it all goes south, it's up to them to rewrite the script, save the castle's future, and find their own happy ending.

Tropes

Small Town, Soulmates, Grumpy/Sunshine, Fish-out-of-Water

KISSING GAMES

Bodyguard Charlie has a new mission: teach workaholic Hollywood actress Valentina how to play, one wild adventure at a time. But when no-strings fun turns into something more, they have to face some hard truths. Can they find a future together, or will their love remain a Highland fling?

Tropes

Small Town, Dark Secrets, Bodyguard/Actress, Forced Proximity, Alpha-roll hero, Dating Game

MUSICAL GAMES

After lying to a Hollywood megastar, Sam needs Jamie to write an album with her in just ten days He's got the voice of an angel and the body of a god, but fame is the last thing on his mind. Will he help make her dreams come true?

Tropes

Small Town, Grumpy/Sunshine, Male Virgin, Cinnamon Roll Hero, Opposites Attract, Fish-out-of-Water, Forced Proximity

WEDDING GAMES

Rory and Zoe want to get married. Not easy when their mothers are mortal enemies and Rory's step-father is a Hollywood star with a death wish. Can they unravel the tangles in time to tie the knot, or is eloping the only answer? Get ready for Scotland's wedding of the year!

Tropes

Small Town, Grumpy/Sunshine, Opposites Attract, Soulmates, Fish-out-of-Water

CHRISTMAS GAMES

Having a baby's easy, right? Until wayward in-laws, an out-of-control cow and mad Santa get in the way. All Rory and Zoe want is a relaxing Christmas before their baby arrives, but straightforward is not their style...

Tropes

Small Town, Grumpy/Sunshine, Opposites Attract, Soulmates, Fish-

❧

THE FOXBROOKE SERIES

ONE NIGHT IN FOXBROOKE

When chef Ben 'Kenobi' Walker gets the call to help save a VIP dinner at Foxbrooke Manor, he doesn't expect to run into old flame Leia Perry. She's all grown up and even more attractive than when they were teenagers – but she hasn't forgotten what happened ten years ago, and she *definitely* hasn't forgiven him. Will one night give Ben the second chance he needs to prove himself and win back Leia's heart?

Tropes

Small Town, Second Chance, Return to Hometown, Enemies-to-Lovers, Bet, Brother's Best Friend, Work Colleagues, Forced Proximity, First Love, Reverse Grumpy-Sunshine, Opposites Attract

LOVE AD LIB

Shy and reserved Lord Henry Foxbrooke needs a fake girlfriend. Free-spirited actress Libby Fletcher needs a job. But when they arrive in Somerset for Henry's birthday celebrations, neither are prepared for their reception. As friendship blurs and faking it starts to feel a little too real, disaster strikes. Can Libby and Henry stick to the script, or has their entire act just bombed?

Tropes

Small Town, Fake Dating, Grumpy/Sunshine, Opposites Attract, One Bed, Different Worlds, Fish-out-of-Water

AN UNHOLY AFFAIR

Gorgeous Jack Newton has fallen in love with Eveline Shaw. But she's a female vicar dreaming of marriage and kids, and he's a male escort heading out of town. Can Jack show Eveline heaven and keep his secret safe, or are they both headed straight for hell?

Tropes

Small Town, Forbidden Love, Love at First Sight, Sworn off a Relationship, Priest, Different Worlds, Opposites Attract, Dark Secret

THE UPPER CRUSH

James Hunter-Savage is a cocky city boy who isn't used to anyone else taking the reins. Lady Estelle Foxbrooke is a fiery country girl who's about to show him who's boss. Can they learn to fight for love rather than with each other, or will their love hate relationship destroy everything they're working for?

Tropes

Small Town, Enemies-to-Lovers, Alpha Hero, Love/Hate, Playboy in Love, Different Worlds, Workplace Romance, Fake Dating

THE LOVE POSITION

Beautiful academic, Sophia Hunter-Savage, has run away to an ashram to reinvent herself. Hot yoga teacher, Isaac Hayward, has left town to avoid the only woman able to tempt him off the spiritual path.

But karma sucks.

Now Isaac's teaching Sophia and they're finding themselves in all kinds of unexpected positions. Will their forbidden love bring inner peace and happiness, or end in a tangled mess?

Tropes

Forbidden Love, Opposites Attract, Teacher/Student, Sworn off a Relationship, Forced Proximity, Love at First Sight, Different Worlds, Fish-out-of-Water

CHRISTMAS OFF SCRIPT

Best friends, Leo Foxbrooke and Ella Chamberlain, have never been single at the same time. Until now... Playing Cinderella and Prince Charming in the Christmas pantomime, their on-stage chemistry kindles an unexpected spark behind the scenes. Can they rewrite their friendship this festive season and finally unwrap true love?

Tropes

Small Town, Friends-to-Lovers, Best Friend's Ex, Oblivious to Love, Unrequited Love, Fake Relationship

ONE NIGHT ONLY

Pop star Avery Taylor craves a break from her public life, and a one-night stand with a stranger feels like the perfect escape. A year later, while recovering from an injury, she's stunned to find her nurse is Connor Foxbrooke, the man who touched her soul that night. Avery is ready to break the rules for love, but Connor, who values his quiet life, fears heartbreak. With Avery set to return to the spotlight as soon as she's recovered, can they bridge their worlds and turn their one night into forever?

Tropes

Second-Chance, Mistaken Identity, One Night Stand, Different Worlds, Opposites Attract, Injury, Forced Proximity, Fish-out-of-Water, Celebrity, Pop Star, Small Town

RIGHTING MR WRONG

Mooning a party of nuns is bad for anyone, but for TV star Aiden Wilder, it's catastrophic. Enter Willow Foxbrooke, a quiet PR worker who's tasked with saving his reputation through a fake relationship. As Willow teaches him how to recover his image, they start to fall for each other. But how can true love grow from something that was never real to begin with?

Tropes

Small Town, Fake Dating, Grumpy/Sunshine, Celebrity, Opposites Attract, Different Worlds, Fish-out-of-Water

UNDER THE INFLUENCER

Sunny Summer Foxbrooke's career as an Influencer is over. Now she's forced to work with grumpy Finn Oakley, the man who's avoided her for years. Will Finn finally return her love, or will she always just be his best friend's little sister?

Tropes

Brother's best friend, Grumpy/Sunshine, Beauty and the Beast, Age Gap, Unrequited Love, Rivals, Different Worlds, All Grown Up, Small Town

৩৬৩

By Evie Alexander and Kelly Kay

EVIE & KELLY'S HOLIDAY DISASTERS SERIES

Evie and Kelly's Holiday Disasters are a series of hot and hilarious romantic comedies with interconnected characters, focusing on one holiday and one trope at a time.

CUPID CALAMITY

Featuring **Animal Attraction** & **Stupid Cupid**

Patrick and Sabina have ditched their blind dates for each other. Ben's fighting a crazed chimp for Laurie's love. Insta-love meets insta-disaster in these laugh-out-loud Valentine's day novellas.

COOKOUT CARNAGE

Featuring **Off With a Bang** & **Up in Smoke**

Cute farm boy Jonathan clings to a love ideal, blissfully ignoring what the universe has planned, while keeping track of his pet pig. Posh Brit follows his heart into the American Midwest in search of Sherilyn, his digital dream love.

CHRISTMAS CHAOS

Featuring **No way in a Manger** & **No Crib and No Bed**

In Scotland, Zoe and Rory attempt to have a civilised and respectable rite of passage, but straightforward is not their style. In Sonoma, Bax and Tabi attempt to throw a meaningful Christmas celebration. But there are too many people involved and it's nothing like they expect.

Get Evie's books in all formats as well as special offers, early releases, and exclusive deals direct from her website:

www.eviealexanderbooks.com

EMLIN
PRESS

ABOUT THE AUTHOR

Evie Alexander is a multi-award-winning author of sexy romantic comedies, blending snort-laugh humour and panty-melting chemistry into unputdownable stories that will steal your heart.

When she's not dreaming up swoony heroes and relatable heroines, Evie can be found in the beautiful West Country of the UK, where she lives with her ridiculously patient husband, miracle daughter, and two dogs who think they run the show.

eviealexanderbooks.com

www.eviealexanderauthor.com